Digging Deep

Also by Elena Delle Donne

Hoops
Elle of the Ball
Full-Court Press
Out of Bounds

My Shot

4

Elena Delle Donne

Simon & Schuster Books for Young Readers
New York London Toronto Sydney New Delhi

SIMON & SCHUSTER BOOKS FOR YOUNG READERS
An imprint of Simon & Schuster Children's Publishing Division
1230 Avenue of the Americas, New York, New York 10020
SIMON & SCHUSTER BOOKS FOR YOUNG READERS is a
trademark of Simon & Schuster, Inc.
For information about special discounts for bulk purchases, please
contact Simon & Schuster Special Sales at 1-866-506-1949 or
business@simonandschuster.com.
The Simon & Schuster Speakers Bureau can bring authors to your
live event. For more information or to book an event, contact the
Simon & Schuster Speakers Bureau at 1-866-248-3049 or visit our
website at www.simonspeakers.com.
Jacket design by Laurent Linn
Interior design by Hilary Zarycky
The text for this book was set in Minister.
Manufactured in the United States of America
0519 FFG
First Edition
2 4 6 8 10 9 7 5 3 1
Library of Congress Cataloging-in-Publication Data
Names: Delle Donne, Elena, author.
Title: Digging deep / Elena Delle Donne.
Description: New York : Simon & Schuster Books for Young
Readers, [2019] |
Series: Hoops ; 4 | Summary: Twelve-year-old Elle, still unsure
about quitting the basketball team, fills in for an injured volleyball
player and is surprised at how much less pressure she feels.
Identifiers: LCCN 2018045654|
ISBN 9781534441248 (hardback) | ISBN 9781534441262 (eBook)
| Subjects: | CYAC: Volleyball—Fiction. | Basketball—Fiction. |
Middle schools—Fiction. | Schools—Fiction. | BISAC: JUVENILE
FICTION / Sports & Recreation / Basketball. | JUVENILE
FICTION / Girls & Women. | JUVENILE
FICTION / Social Issues / Self-Esteem & Self-Reliance.
Classification: LCC PZ7.1.D4558 Dig 2019 | DDC [Fic]—dc23
LC record available at https://lccn.loc.gov/2018045654

For my goddaughter, Gia,

and all the young ballers out there

Acknowledgments

I have a team of people that I would like to thank, and I fully recognize that I would not be where I am today without the support of my family and friends behind me.

Amanda, my wife and my best friend, you have given up and sacrificed so much to help me better my career (even being my off-season workout partner). Words cannot express how much you mean to me, and I am so excited that you are with me for life. We are a pretty unstoppable team.

Special thanks to my incredible parents, who have been with me since day one. Mom, thank you for being extremely honest, absolutely hilarious, and my ultimate role model for what strength looks like.

Dad, thank you for driving me all the way to Pennsylvania twice a week, attending every AAU tournament, and still traveling to lots of my WNBA games. You are my biggest fan.

To my older sister, Lizzie, thank you for helping me keep everything in perspective. You remind me that there is so much more to life, and that joys can come from anywhere—even something as simple as the wind or a perfectly cooked rib eye. You are the greatest gift to our family. And thanks to my big brother, Gene, for being able to make me laugh, especially through the lows, and for being my biggest cheerleader.

Wrigley, my greatest friend and Greatest Dane. Thanks for being my rock in Chicago and for attacking me with love every time I come home. Rasta, thanks for being the edge and sass in our home and for being the only one in our house who can keep Amanda in check.

Erin Kane and Alyssa Romano, thank you for helping me discover myself and for helping me find my voice. This wouldn't have happened without the greatest team behind me.

Thanks to my Octagon literary agent, Jennifer Keene, for all her great work on this project. Thanks to the all-stars at Simon & Schuster, including Liz Kossnar.

Thank you all.

Time for Something New?

In my dream I was tearing down the basketball court, dribbling so fast past the defenders that they were just a blur. The crowd chanted my name. "Elle! Elle! Elle! Elle!"

I approached the basket and jumped up, my body feeling light as I floated upward, ready to dunk. I flew high above the basket, but when I looked down, I didn't see net. I saw a dark, swirling tunnel of wind.

"Nooooooo!" I yelled as the tunnel sucked me inside. My body twisted and turned as I plummeted down into the tunnel, about to . . .

"Zobe, no!" I cried. My Great Dane was licking my face as I sprang awake, my heart pounding from the dream.

I thought I knew what the dream meant. On Friday I had quit the school basketball team. Today was Monday, and I'd have to face most of my teammates for the first time since I'd walked out. I was pretty nervous about that.

I pulled my covers over my head. Zobe nudged them aside with his big doggy nose. I knew he wanted his morning walk, and breakfast.

"Can't we just stay home today, Zobe?" I asked him. "Let's just stay right here in this bed."

"Woof!" Zobe gave a loud, deep bark. I sighed and threw off the covers. Zobe was not going to let me win this argument.

Twenty minutes later Zobe was eating his kibble and I was eating my cereal, nervously tapping my foot on the floor.

Mom sat down next to me and plunked her steaming coffee mug on the table. "Jim's going to drive you and Blake to school this week. I'll be picking you both up, except on days when Blake has basketball practice, or when you're staying late for the anti-bully club, or Camp Cooperation. Then I'll just get you."

I nodded. Jim is my older brother, Blake is one of my best friends, and we all go to Spring Meadow, a private school in Wilmington, Delaware. We live in Greenmont, which is about thirty minutes away. And now that Jim is a senior, and has his own car, he helps out sometimes.

"What am I doing?" Jim asked, yawning as he walked into the kitchen.

"I believe you are driving Elle and Blake to school," Dad said, not looking up from his laptop. He owns a real-estate business in Wilmington, and he works a lot. Even during breakfast!

"Cool," Jim said, and I felt grateful that he wasn't the kind of older brother who would complain about taking his little sister to school.

Actually, I'm not sure if the phrase "little sister" can technically apply to me. I'm twelve years old and six feet tall. So I'm not very little. It's one of the reasons I started playing basketball in the first place.

It's also one of the reasons I quit.

Jim grabbed a protein bar from the cabinet. "You ready, Elle?"

I jumped up from my seat. "Yes!" I put my dishes in the sink and then moved over to my sister, Beth, who was sitting in her wheelchair at the end of the table.

I leaned over and let Beth sniff my head so she would know it was me, because she couldn't see or hear me. Then I took her hand and traced two symbols onto her palm with my finger, part of the special language that we used to communicate with her.

Good-bye. Love.

Beth took my hand and answered me. *Love.*

"I'll be at the pickup area at three," Mom told me.

"Thanks," I said, and inside I was thinking, *Three, not five, because I'm not going to basketball practice. Weird!* I was going to have to get used to my new Monday routine.

I walked outside with Jim and saw Blake making a beeline for Jim's car in the driveway.

"Shotgun!" I yelled, and dashed to the front passenger seat side of the car.

"Not fair!" Blake protested.

"Of course it's fair," I said. "I called it."

Blake couldn't argue with that. Those shotgun rules had a history going back to when we had both grown tall enough to sit in the front seat. He frowned and slid into the back. I got into the passenger side and then, to bust him, I pushed the seat back as far as it would go.

"Hey, now that's definitely not fair!" Blake cried.

Jim shook his head. "Are you two twelve or five?" he asked.

I quickly pulled up my seat and locked in my seat belt. I heard Blake yawn behind me.

"I hate Mondays," he complained as Jim pulled the car out of the driveway.

"I hate *this* Monday," I said. "I haven't seen anybody since I quit the team, except for you and Avery."

Avery is my other best friend. She and I played on the girls' basketball team together, the Nighthawks. Pretty much everybody I hang out with in school is on the team.

"You think it will be a big deal?" my brother asked.

"I *know* it will," I groaned.

"You might be right," Blake said. "Bianca's been texting me all weekend, freaking out."

"Really?" I asked. "I thought she'd be thrilled. She hated it when Coach Ramirez made me center."

"Well, she's happy she's center," Blake admitted, "but she's worried about the team. She wants to make it to the championships. And she doesn't think the Nighthawks can get there without you."

"Of course they can," I said quickly, but that was followed by a pang of doubt. I hadn't really thought about the fact that my leaving could hurt the team's record. That they might lose without me.

They won't, I told myself. *They've got too many good players.* Bianca was really good. So was Avery, and Tiff and Dina were pretty solid. They didn't need me.

That didn't stop me from feeling guilty though, especially when we got to school and my friends Hannah and Natalie ambushed me at my locker. They both squashed me in a double hug.

"Elle, please don't quit!" cried pink-haired Natalie

as they pulled away from me. "I thought you loved basketball more than any of us!"

"I still love basketball," I said. "I just don't feel comfortable playing it competitively right now."

"What can we do to get you to stay?" Hannah asked. I felt awful, because her big brown eyes looked so sad when she said it.

"Nothing," I said. "I mean, thanks, but this is just something I need to do. It's not personal."

Hannah sighed. "I thought you would say that."

"I get it," Natalie added. "As long as you're happy, Elle."

"Thanks," I replied, although I wasn't sure if I was happy, exactly. Relieved, maybe. But I hadn't gotten to "happy" yet.

Next, Bianca walked by with her best friend, Tiff. Bianca didn't say a word to me; she just tossed her glossy black hair as she passed and glared at me. Tiff, who was wearing a blue hijab over her dark brown hair, shot me a look of apology.

Luckily, Avery was right behind them. She stopped and grabbed my arm.

"You all right?" she asked.

I nodded. "Just walk with me to homeroom, okay?"

"Sure," Avery said.

I'm glad I asked her, because even though it was a short walk, I passed all the rest of my teammates.

"You can't *really* be quitting, Elle," Dina said, talking fast as she kept pace with us. "Say it's not true."

"It's true," I replied, and Dina stopped following us and shook her head.

Patrice looked up at me from her locker and just nodded. The coach's daughter, she had almost quit too, a week ago. She kind of looked like she wanted to talk to me, but she didn't say anything.

Then Caroline walked up to me and Avery.

"I'm going to miss you on the team, Elle," she said.

"Yeah, me too," I said. "But I'll still see you at Camp Cooperation!"

Caroline and I both volunteer for this after-school program for kids with special needs.

Then Avery turned the corner and literally bumped into the last (but definitely not least) member of the team, Amanda. She smiled at me, and I smiled back. But seeing Amanda always makes me smile.

"Hey, guys," she said. "Elle, I mean it. We need to go on a doggy date this weekend."

I laughed. "I definitely want to," I said. Amanda has a dog too—an English springer spaniel named Freckles. "I just need to check my scheduling app. Even without basketball, I still seem to have a packed schedule."

"Make sure to squeeze me in," Amanda said with a grin, and then we all stepped into homeroom together and took our seats as the bell rang.

"Good morning, Spring Meadow students and staff!" Principal Lubin's morning voice, always cheerful, rang out over the school sound system. "I'm wearing my sunglasses to school today and do you know why? Because the students here at Spring Meadow are so bright!"

Everybody in class groaned. Principal Lubin's puns were always painful, but he was a really nice principal, so we all forgave him for it.

"I'm proud to reannounce that Ms. Ebear is organizing the Buddy Club, an anti-bullying club in the middle school that will meet after school on Wednesdays," he said. "This club is open to all students in grades six through eight. We're currently working on a club for elementary school students that will meet during lunch period. Stay tuned for more details, and if you haven't already, look for the sign-up sheet for Ms. Ebear's club in the middle school front hallway."

Then we said the Pledge of Allegiance, and the speaker crackled off. Besides being the advisor for the anti-bullying club, Ms. Ebear was also our homeroom and World History teacher, and my favorite. She wore her shiny brown hair in a neat bob, and she had kind green eyes behind her severe black eyeglasses.

"I need to thank Principal Lubin for that shout-out," she said. "And I hope to see some of you in this class at our meeting on Wednesday."

Avery leaned toward me. "I wish I could go, but we—I mean, I—have basketball practice."

I nodded, feeling guilty. I was planning to join Ms. Ebear's club. In fact, learning about it was one of the reasons I had decided to quit basketball. Avery had been really supportive of my decision to quit, but I felt bad telling her that I was joining the club when I knew she couldn't—so I didn't say anything.

After homeroom I stayed in the room for World History class with Ms. Ebear. Nobody talked to me about quitting the basketball team, which was a relief. Same in second period science class. But then came third period gym.

I had changed into my green gym shirt and shorts and was leaving the locker room when Kenya and Maggie approached me. I know them because Spring Meadow is a small school, but I've never really hung out with them. They were both athletic—and both on the girls' volleyball team.

"I heard you quit basketball," Kenya said.

"Yeah," I replied. Where was this going?

"We need your help on the volleyball team," Kenya continued. "Lauren sprained her wrist and we're down a player until she gets better. And we've seen you play in gym and we know you're good."

Maggie hadn't said anything yet—I knew she

was quiet—but she stared at me with intense blue eyes that peered out from under her blond bangs.

"Oh wow, I don't know what to say," I replied. "I mean, I like volleyball. But I . . . when are the practices?"

"Tuesdays after school, and Fridays at five," Kenya replied. "And then a game every Friday at seven."

I bit my lip, thinking. The schedule was definitely less stressful than the basketball schedule. It still left me free to volunteer on Thursdays, and to join Ms. Ebear's club. I had loved playing volleyball in gym class. And it would only be temporary, until Lauren's wrist healed. Still . . .

"I need to think about it," I said.

"Don't think too hard," Kenya told me. "If you decide to do it, come to practice tomorrow."

I nodded. "Okay," I said.

Avery walked up to me. "What was that about?" she asked.

"Oh, nothing," I said. Once again, I felt awkward telling Avery I might be doing something cool instead of basketball. Avery looked at me suspiciously, but she didn't press me.

I thought about Kenya's offer as I jogged around the gym. One reason I had quit basketball was because it was getting stressful. Coach Ramirez expected a lot from me. Would volleyball be the same? I wondered.

I jogged past Bianca and Dina. Dina nodded to me, but Bianca deliberately looked the other way.

What was her deal? Bianca had been mad when Coach Ramirez had given me her position on the team, and the pressure and taunting I'd gotten from Bianca was another reason I'd quit. But even though I wasn't on the team anymore, nothing had gotten better. I'd thought maybe she'd be nicer to me once I left, but obviously I was wrong about that.

I glanced back at the volleyball girls. Was one of them another Bianca? Would I be walking from one bad situation into another?

That's not the only reason you quit, I reminded myself. One of the main reasons was because it felt like my height had sentenced me to play basketball . . . forever. People were already telling me that I was on a track to become a pro player, and I was only twelve! What if I wanted to do something different with my life? If I didn't find out now, when would I?

You love sports, I told myself. *Why not give volleyball a try?*

That question bounced around in my head all day. I decided to ask my parents about it at dinner, and when I did they were thrilled, which surprised me a little bit.

"I think it's a great idea to try something new!" Dad said.

Mom nodded. "I was worried that you were just going to be moping around, Elle. I know you're joining the anti-bullying club, but that's only one day a week, and basketball was such a big commitment."

"The volleyball schedule is easier," I said. "I can help out the team and still have time to try some new things."

"It seems like a good idea," Mom agreed. "But are you sure that you won't have the same issues with volleyball that you did with basketball? I hated seeing the way the pressure got to you, Elle."

I shrugged. "I have no idea, because I've never been on a volleyball team before. All I know is basketball. But I think maybe it's worth finding out. And the team needs me—I'd really be helping them out."

"Fair enough," Mom replied. "So have you decided?"

I took a deep breath. "Yeah. I'm going to do it."

"Great!" Mom said. "E-mail me your new practice and game schedule."

After dinner I saw I had a text on my phone from an unknown number. It was Kenya.

Got your number from Blake. Did you decide? We have practice tomorrow.

Wow, she's persistent, I thought. It was kind of flattering, though.

See you at practice, I typed back. **I'll join the team until Lauren is better!!**

Serve It, Serve It, Do Not Swerve It!

I felt really happy and excited after I'd sent the text to Kenya. I started to write a text to Avery to share the good news, and then I stopped.

Maybe I wouldn't tell her. Not yet.

So the next morning I didn't say anything to Blake when Jim drove us to school. And I didn't tell Avery during homeroom.

Then, at lunchtime, I had to come clean.

I sat with Avery, Hannah, Natalie, Caroline, and Patrice, as usual. I was eating the salad that Mom had packed for me and laughing at Natalie's impression of a video game streamer—one of those guys online with millions of followers—when Amanda walked up.

"Hey, Elle," she said. "If you want, my mom could give you a ride home from school with me. And we could walk the dogs together."

"Oh wow," I said. I'd meant to set up a doggy date with her, but I'd forgotten. "I would love to, but I can't. I'm . . . I'm busy."

I couldn't go because I had volleyball practice, but I didn't want to say that out loud. So I picked up my cell phone. A few weeks ago I'd had a meltdown because my responsibilities had gotten out of control. Avery had installed a scheduling app on my phone, U-Plan.

"I, um, my scheduling app says I need to study," I said.

Amanda frowned. "Aw, okay. Maybe some other time."

Before I could stop her, Avery took the phone from me.

"You know, Elle, you can switch around blocks in your schedule," she said. She tapped the screen.

"See? You can switch your study time this afternoon with your free time before dinner, like this."

I was relieved that I hadn't programmed volleyball practice into the app yet—but that relief didn't last long.

Amanda's face brightened. "Great! So we're on for our doggy date?"

My face felt hot. "Actually, I have something else planned," I said. "I'm . . . I'm going to volleyball practice."

Avery's eyes widened. Hannah and Natalie stopped talking and stared at me. Caroline and Patrice exchanged surprised looks. And Amanda's mouth dropped open.

"I didn't mean to lie about it," I told Amanda. "I just . . . wasn't ready to tell everybody about it yet."

"Is *that* why you quit the team?" Natalie asked. "So you could play volleyball?"

"No!" I said quickly. "It's not like that. I had a lot of reasons."

"Like playing volleyball," Natalie said.

I turned to Avery. "You know that I didn't plan

this, right? Kenya and Maggie asked me yesterday to fill in for a little while, because one of their teammates is hurt. It just sounded like fun."

"Sure," Avery said. But she didn't sound exactly like she believed me.

Amanda's smile returned. "Cool, Elle," she said. "You should do what makes you happy. And the volley-ball team is lucky to have you. Just promise me you'll find a place in your phone for us to hang out, okay?"

"I promise!" I said, and she walked away.

"My mom always says to follow your bliss," Avery said. "So go for it, Elle."

"Thanks," I said, but I saw Natalie roll her eyes at Hannah, and neither of them spoke to me for the whole rest of lunch.

I knew that they were probably mad at me for joining volleyball so soon after quitting basketball, which bummed me out. But I still felt excited when the last bell of the day rang and it was time for volleyball practice.

I headed into the middle school gym. Immediately, Kenya, Maggie, and three other girls—Summer,

Taylor, and Jenna—ran up to me and crushed me in a group hug.

"Elle! You're saving us!" cried Summer.

"Thanks, Elle!" said Taylor.

"Welcome to the team," Jenna said.

All five girls were dressed in green T-shirts with "Spring Meadow Volleyball Club" on the back in yellow letters, and green shorts with yellow stripes. They all wore their long hair in ponytails: Kenya's dark brown hair, Maggie's pale blond hair, Summer's golden blond hair, Taylor's light brown hair, and Jenna's black hair. Kenya, Maggie, Summer, and Taylor were all about five-foot-six, while Jenna was shorter and more muscular.

"Thanks," I said, happy to get a warm welcome. I held up my gym bag. "I wasn't sure what to wear. Is my gym uniform okay?"

Kenya nodded. "Coach Patel has a uniform for you." She looked down at my sneakers. "You might want to pick up some shoes especially made for volleyball before Friday, if you have time."

"These are Apex Nitros," Summer said, holding

up facing our partners, one at the net and the other at the ten-foot line.

"So, you all should know that a team can only hit the ball three times before it goes to the other side of the net, and no player can hit the ball two consecutive times," Coach Patel began. "Ideally, what we're looking for are three different types of hits: the pass, the set, and the spike."

This was a lot more than Coach Patel had ever explained in class. I knew the basic rules, but as far as I knew, you just had to hit the ball to the other side as hard as you could without the ball going out of bounds.

"Maggie and Summer, demonstrate passing," Coach instructed.

Both girls got into position, their legs shoulder-width apart and knees bent. They extended both arms.

"To pass, you make a fist with your nondominant hand and cover it with your dominant hand," Coach said, demonstrating. Maggie and Summer did the same, and I bent my knees, getting into position like the others.

out her leg to show me her shoe. "They've got nc
bottoms, and gel support for jumping and lanc

"Oh, okay." I said. I hadn't thought about nec
special shoes for volleyball. I'd always thought
being less complicated than basketball.

I was about to find out how wrong I was. ﹒
we changed, we all went back out into the ﹗
where Coach Patel was waiting for us. Before tc
I knew him as *Mr.* Patel, my gym teacher.

"First of all, welcome to the team, Elle," he ﹗
"We need six members to keep this little club tc
alive, and Lauren's injury would have put us ou
competition. So we're very glad you're joining us

The other girls whooped and cheered, and t
all high-fived me.

"Now, Elle, I've seen you play in gym, an
know you can play this game," Coach Patel sa
"But we do things a little more structured
competitive play, so today we're going to bri
you up to speed with some basic drills. Everybo
pair up, please! Kenya, you partner with Elle."

I followed the lead of the other girls and we lin

"Keep your forearms together," Coach went on. "They'll create a platform for the ball. When the ball comes to you, don't swing your arms. Don't hit it with your hands or wrist. Let the ball hit the platform and control it, using your legs to power it to where you want to go."

He tossed a volleyball at Maggie. She let it meet her "platform" and sent it sailing toward Summer, who passed it back to her the same way.

"All right now, everybody," Coach said. He tossed a ball to Jenna, and then to Kenya, who passed the ball to me. I moved toward the ball and instinctively swung my arms up. I frowned as the ball went rocketing out of control.

"Don't swing, Elle," Coach said, and I nodded. Kenya passed the ball to me again, and this time I did a little better. We kept going back and forth until I got the hang of it.

"You got it, Elle!" Kenya said with a grin, and I felt a wave of satisfaction wash over me. This was fun!

Next, we learned about setting. That's when you guide the ball as high as you can and get it into position for the hitters, who are usually by the front of the net. To start, you bend your knees and extend your arms above your head with your palms facing up and your fingers spread out wide, like you're holding a two-liter bottle of soda. Then you push up on the ball to send it high.

"Your legs are also what will give the ball power when you are setting," Coach Patel said. "Not just your wrists."

I nodded. "It's kind of like shooting a basketball."

Maybe it was all the basketball shooting I'd done, but I got the hang of setting pretty quickly. Kenya and I set the ball back and forth, moving farther and farther apart on Coach's word.

The last move was the trickiest—and also the most fun. That's the third hit, when you ideally spike the ball over the net to crash down quickly and land somewhere that the players have to scramble to reach. It's called a kill if no one can pass it up.

Kenya and Taylor demonstrated spiking for me, starting at the ten-foot line.

"I like to take three steps," Kenya said. "The first

one gets me in the right direction. The second one gives me power." As she took this step, she moved her right foot in front of her left, leaned forward, and extended her arms behind her.

"And the third step finishes it, so you can jump as high as you can," Kenya said. Her left leg joined her right leg, and her arms swung forward and up to hit the ball.

Taylor lobbed the ball to a height above the net, and Kenya demonstrated the move again, this time spiking the ball over the net.

I tried to copy her movements. "I need to remember to lean forward," I said. "In gym I always just hit it over the net without thinking about my form."

"Don't worry. You'll get it," Summer told me.

We all practiced spiking then. Finally, Coach Patel had us practice serving—something I already knew I was pretty good at.

"Serve it, serve it, do not swerve it!" Taylor and Jenna chanted before we began.

"That's right," Coach said. "Serving is all about control."

As we practiced, everybody was doing their best—but also smiling and laughing. Coach Patel's comments always came across as positive and helpful.

"Try that footwork again, Elle. But keep up that great energy!"

"Good power on that serve, Jenna. Just try for some better control next time!"

Practice seemed to fly by, and before I knew it, it was time go to, and I was climbing into Mom's car.

"How do you feel?" she asked.

"Sweaty," I replied. "And I think I used muscles that I didn't know I had."

Mom laughed.

Then I thought about my new teammates, and how friendly and supportive they'd been. And how much fun we'd had, and how nice Mr. Patel was as a coach.

"But mostly, I feel happy," I told her.

Have You Ever Been Bullied?

R aise your hand if you've ever been bullied," Ms. Ebear said.

Five of us had come to Ms. Ebear's room for the first meeting of the Buddy Club. When she asked the question, one kid's hand shot up—Dylan, who's in seventh grade with me and who was my partner when we had to do this dumb, mandatory school dance in September.

The rest of us just kind of looked at one another and the floor. Dylan was the only one I knew well. Cole was class president of the eighth grade, one of those kids who's in every group and club. The other two, Gabrielle and Katie, were in sixth grade, and I didn't know them very well.

I didn't raise my hand right away because I wasn't sure if I should. I mean, I'd had kids be mean to me before, but I wasn't exactly sure if that meant I'd been bullied.

Cole raised his hand. "Ms. Ebear, what exactly do you mean by bullying? I mean, is it like when somebody beats you up?"

"That is one way you can be bullied," she said. Then she moved to a poster on the wall, a new one I hadn't seen in her classroom before. Across the top were the words: WHAT IS BULLYING? And underneath was a long list of types of bullying.

"Bullying can be physical, when somebody hits, pushes, or trips you," Ms. Ebear said. "Or when they take your things from you, or break your things."

"Like when somebody pushes your books out of your arms when you're walking down the hall," said Gabrielle.

"That's right," Ms. Ebear said. "Then there is

emotional bullying, when somebody calls you names, laughs at you, or leaves you out of an activity on purpose to try to make you feel bad about who you are. Spreading lies or rumors is also a form of emotional bullying."

I thought of the player on the Bobcats who'd called me Big Bird on the court. And all the times I'd been teased because of my height. I raised my hand. "I guess I've been bullied, then."

Gabrielle looked surprised. "Really? But you're so popular, Elle. You're a basketball star, and tall, and blond . . ."

"You just said it. *Tall*," I said. "People have made fun of my height since I was little."

"Me too," Dylan said. "But I have the *opposite* problem that you do."

Everyone knew what he meant. Dylan was the shortest kid in the room—not to mention the whole seventh grade.

Katie raised her hand. "What kind of bullying is cyberbullying?"

"It's a form of emotional bullying too," Ms. Ebear

replied. "Cyberbullying is when somebody sends mean texts, or posts negative or mean things online about someone. Even liking a mean comment about someone is a form of bullying."

"That is just awful," said Gabrielle. "Cyberbullying is the worst, because people are *way* meaner online than they are to one another in person."

"I believe that's true," Ms. Ebear agreed. "Spring Meadow is a pretty friendly school, and we've got a very clear policy against bullying—any kind of bullying. But in the last few years, I've noticed that bullying has increased here in the middle school. So this club is a way to try to stop that. I'm really glad that the five of you are here today. We're off to a great start!"

"So are we going to be like the anti-bullying squad, or something?" Cole asked. "Like, reporting people for bullying?"

"Not exactly," Ms. Ebear replied. "I think I'd like us to decide as a group how we want to move forward. The first step would be for us all to learn about the best ways to stop bullying when we see it.

In that way, I guess you could say that we *would* be an anti-bullying squad."

"Bully Busters," Dylan joked.

"That's pretty cute, but there's a reason why I named this group the Buddy Club," Ms. Ebear explained. "I believe that friendship is the cure to the bullying crisis. When people have friends who support them, they are less likely to become victims of bullying. And some bullies are kids who are lonely, with problems of their own, and they need a support system too."

"There are only five of us," Gabrielle said. "Are we supposed to make friends with everybody in the school?"

"It just takes one person to make a difference," Ms. Ebear said. "If each one of us reaches out to somebody who needs a friend, that's a good start."

"Maybe it'll be contagious," Dylan added. "You know, like, I'll make one friend, and that person will make a friend, and then that person will make a friend, and it'll keep going."

Ms. Ebear laughed. "That sounds like a good

kind of contagious," she said. "Maybe this week we could each think about one person we know who could use a buddy, and reach out to them. Have a conversation. Invite them to eat lunch with you. You don't have to become best friends, but a small gesture can go a long way."

I started thinking about who I knew who might need a buddy, and I thought about Patrice. I guess she had the basketball team as her support system, but she didn't really hang out with anybody except at practice and the games. Maybe it was because she was the coach's daughter. Or because she was naturally quiet and shy; I wasn't sure. But I had always meant to get to know her better. If I needed to make a buddy for the Buddy Club, then Patrice seemed like a good person to start with.

"So, since this is our first meeting, let's get to know one another a little better," Ms. Ebear said. "Why did you come today?"

"As you know, I'm the eighth-grade class president," Cole replied. "I'm here to help improve the quality of life for the eighth graders of Spring Meadow School."

He sounds like a politician, I thought. But I knew he was nice to other kids in school—and a decent player on the boys' basketball team.

"Katie and I are Girl Scouts," Gabrielle said. "A few months ago we decided to try to get an anti-bullying badge, and when we saw the club, we thought it was . . ."

". . . destiny!" Katie finished for her.

"I was a Girl Scout," Ms. Ebear said. "I'd love to see what the badge requirements are. Maybe we can use them to help guide our activities."

"Sure," Gabriella replied.

Ms. Ebear turned to me. "What about you, Elle?"

"Well, I guess the main reason is because of my sister, Beth," I said. "She's got special needs. She's in a wheelchair and can't see or hear, and she's got cerebral palsy and autism. I've met a lot of special needs kids through Beth, and I know a lot of them get bullied. And that's something I just don't understand."

"That's awful!" Katie cried. "What kind of person makes fun of someone with special needs?"

"I don't know," I said. "It makes no sense to

me. I mean, call me beanpole or ask me what the weather's like up here, if you want. I can take it. But why would you make fun of someone who has so many other challenges in life?"

"Because you're a horrible person," Gabrielle answered.

"Or maybe you're hurting really bad inside," Dylan said.

Ms. Ebear hopped off her desk. "Wow, I can tell this is going to be a great group!" she said. "Let's meet here again next week, all right?"

We left Ms. Ebear's room and walked outside. Spring Meadow School is made up of three buildings: one for the elementary school, one for the middle school, and one for the high school. The main pickup and drop-off point is by the high-school front entrance. You can get there by walking all the way around the outside of the high-school building, but I usually took a shortcut through the building, coming in the back entrance.

As soon as I stepped inside the high school, I regretted it. I knew I'd have to walk past the main gym—where my old basketball team was practicing. I felt a pang of something—not guilt, exactly, but a feeling that I should be with them.

I decided to jog past, knowing they'd be too busy practicing to notice me. But I didn't count on seeing Avery in the hallway, filling up her water bottle in the water fountain.

"Elle?" she said. "What are you—you didn't change your mind, did you?"

"No, I, um, I went to Ms. Ebear's meeting," I told her.

Avery nodded. "Oh yeah," she said. "I guess you have time for that now. How was it? And why didn't you tell me you were going?"

"I decided at the last minute," I said. "And it was good. I'll tell you about it tomorrow."

"Sure," Avery said. "I'd better get back, anyway, before Coach Ramirez freaks."

"Yeah," I said, and then Avery ran inside the gym and I continued jogging to the front entrance.

Was that awkward? It felt awkward, I worried, as I waited outside for Mom.

The one thing I didn't want to happen when I quit basketball was for it to hurt my friendship with Avery. She'd been my best friend since first grade. We had survived elementary school together, even when Pamela Johnson had come to school in second grade and wanted Avery to be her best friend. We'd survived Avery discovering she loved to wear dresses and me discovering that I hated wearing them. We'd even survived the Great Fight of Fifth Grade, when Avery thought I had laughed when Michael Fitzgerald had put gum in her hair, but I hadn't—I had actually sneezed.

We'd survived all those things; so we could survive me quitting basketball, right?

I hope so, I thought. *Because Avery is one buddy I do not want to lose!*

Ace!

Elle, you have a volleyball game today against East Lewiston.

I woke up on Friday morning and saw the message pop up from my scheduling app. It was hard to believe I was going to compete in my first volleyball game after I had just joined the team!

I sat up in bed, thinking. On the morning of a basketball game, I had a routine. I would walk Zobe, shoot some hoops, eat half a bagel with peanut butter for energy, nap, and then put my basketball shoes on before I put on my shorts, stepping through the shorts with my right foot so I could start off the game on the right foot. It was my own silly superstition, but I'd based it on the routines of some of my favorite WNBA players.

Did I need to come up with a special routine for volleyball? It wasn't exactly the same. Different sport, for one thing. For another, the game wasn't until seven at night, after school and volleyball practice. And also, every basketball game felt serious. I always felt pressure about how well I'd play. But I wasn't feeling that same pressure about volleyball. It felt different . . . easier.

"Woof!" Zobe's bark got me out of my thoughts. I quickly changed into my school clothes (jeans, a T-shirt, and sneakers) and took Zobe for his morning walk. Then I had a regular morning getting ready for school.

"You want to come over tonight?" Blake asked as he climbed into the back seat of Jim's car. "I got Street Match XV yesterday. The avatar options are awesome."

"Really? Because they never have any cool female ones," I said.

"They fixed that," Blake told me. "This time the number of male and female players is equal. And the coolest one is this girl with dreads and supertoned muscles."

"Woman," I corrected him. "Anyway, I would love to, but I can't. I've got a volleyball game at seven."

"Volleyball?" Blake asked, and then he nodded. "Oh right, Kenya asked me for your number."

"How do you know her, anyway?" I asked.

"We were in day camp together when I was younger," he replied. "She's nice. So you're definitely on the team? Cool."

"It's the club team," I said. "It's not a big deal."

Jim chimed in. "Sure it is," he said. "Where's the game tonight? I'll come cheer you on."

"East Lewiston," I replied. "At the middle school."

"Can you give me a ride?" Blake asked Jim. "I'll go too."

"Sure," Jim said. "We'll leave at six-thirty."

I could feel my body tense up. "You guys don't have to come," I said quickly. "I mean, it's my first game and I've only been to one practice. I could be terrible at it."

"You're a great athlete. You won't be terrible," Jim said.

"Yeah, anyway, it'll be fun to watch a volleyball game for a change," Blake added.

I relaxed a little bit. "Right," I said. "Fun."

We got to the school at the same time Avery's mom dropped her off.

"Hey, Avery," Blake greeted her. "Jim and I are going to Elle's volleyball game tonight. Want to come?"

Avery frowned. "Tonight?" she repeated. "I don't know. We've got practice, and I don't know if I could get there on time."

"Don't worry about it!" I said.

Avery looked relieved. "Thanks," she said. "A game already, huh?"

"Well, I joined the club team midseason," I explained. "They've already been playing games. If I hadn't joined them, they'd have to end the season early. So I'm mostly doing it so the other five girls can compete."

"They're lucky to have you on the team," Avery said, and I heard something in her voice. Sadness? Or was she annoyed? It was hard to tell.

"You know I wasn't planning on joining another sport, right?" I asked. "It's only temporary, until Lauren gets better." I shrugged. "Anyway, it's kind of fun."

Avery gave me a little smile. "I know, Elle. I'm happy for you," she said. But she still sounded sad.

I was psyched for the game that night. I'd had fun at practice on Tuesday. But I was starting to wonder if my life could really be fun if I didn't have basketball—or my friends.

"Today we will give Elle a crash course in volleyball team positions," Coach Patel said, starting off our five o'clock practice. "Then we're going to work on blocking and serving before we head to East Lewiston."

"Positions?" I asked. "You mean, like, the front of the net and back of the net?"

"There are specific positions on a volleyball team,

just like in other sports," Coach Patel explained. "Each position has a specific job on the team, such as setting the ball for the attackers, or blocking the opponent."

"So your position you play depends on where you are on the court," I said slowly, figuring it out. "But we rotate spots after each point, right? Does that mean everyone gets to play a different position during the game?"

"That's how we play," Kenya said. "Starting in high school, some players will always play the same position, no matter where they are on the court."

I frowned. "Wow, that's kind of confusing."

"It doesn't have to be," Summer said. "It all comes down to just getting the ball over the net, and not letting the ball hit the floor when it comes to you."

Coach smiled. "Yes, basically. But it's a good idea to know the positions, so let's go over them." He nodded to the court. "Line up by the net. Three in front and three in back. Any order."

We scrambled onto the court and I ended up in the line at the back. Facing the net, Summer,

Maggie, and Taylor were in front of me, from left to right. I was behind Summer, Jenna was behind Maggie, and Kenya was behind Taylor, in the serving position.

"Kenya is in position one," Coach began. "You know that as the serving position. The player in this position is also known as the setter. The setter keeps the ball in play, and she can attack, too."

"So can anybody attack from any position?" I asked.

"Yes!" Jenna cried, and she jumped up and smacked an imaginary ball over the net. "Yeah, right in the gap!"

Coach Patel walked up to Taylor, who was in front of Kenya.

"Taylor is in position two. The player in this position is known as the right side blocker or the ride side hitter, depending on whether the team is defending or on offense," he said. "All three players in the front of the net need to be good blockers, which is why we'll be practicing that soon."

He walked in front of Maggie.

"Maggie is in position three; and Jenna, behind her, is in position six," he said. "They are middle blockers if the team is defending, or middle hitters if the team is on offense."

"But my position is also called a libero," Jenna said.

"Here she goes," Summer teased.

Jenna turned to me. "It's a special position created in the 1990s. Starting in high school, a libero wears a different-colored jersey. She plays mostly defense and can swap in for a player in the back row when the ball's not in play, and the coach doesn't have to do an official swap. I'm gonna play libero."

"That's because you can't block!" Taylor teased, and Jenna laughed. I was starting to figure out that everybody on the team dogged one another, and nobody minded. Everybody was super chill.

"Maybe I can't block, but I've got fast reflexes," Jenna said, and she did a quick dance move and a spin to prove it.

"The libero has to be a good passer, because the ball often ends up there after a serve," Coach Patel continued. "Elle, the served ball often ends up in your corner too."

"So if Jenna's position six, then I'm position five?" I asked.

"Right. And I'm four," Summer said.

"Positions four and five are outside hitters," Coach Patel said. "In position four, you'll do more blocking."

"And in position five, more passing," I said. "Got it. I think."

Then something hit me. "How do you guys practice positions? I mean, there are only six of us. We can't scrimmage." *Like we did in basketball*, I finished silently.

Maggie shrugged. "We figure it out when we play."

"Yeah, we know it would be better to have more players," Summer said. "But we really wanted to form the club team, and Mr. Patel said he'd coach us, and as long we have six, we're in."

"Yeah, it's better to play than not to play," Taylor said.

I liked what I was hearing. Nobody was talking about winning or crushing the competition.

Everybody was playing because they loved the sport.

"Cool," I said.

"Back row, move to the other side of the net," Coach Patel said. "We're going to practice blocking. Elle, this should be something you're good at because"—I expected him to say *you're tall,* but he didn't—"of your basketball training," he finished.

Coach was right. I picked up the blocking moves pretty quickly: body facing the net. Knees bent. Arms bent at the elbows in front of you, almost like a mime. Palms facing forward and fingers spread wide. When the ball comes, you jump up and extend your arms over the top of the net—easy to do when you're six feet tall, like I am.

After we got the basic moves down, Coach Patel showed us some footwork steps we could use if we needed to move in the direction of the ball. The important thing, I learned, was to always end up facing the net with your palms pointed straight ahead—otherwise, you risked sending the ball out of bounds or falling into the net.

We practiced blocking for so long that we didn't

have time to practice serving. Coach Patel got us all into the school van and took us to East Lewiston for the game. The basketball team was too big to fit in the van, but it was just right for volleyball.

The basketball team might have done cheers or chants on the ride to the game, but as soon as Coach Patel backed out of his space, Taylor started belting out a popular song.

"You're exploding like a fiiiiiirework!"

"That's not how it goes," Summer said.

"Fiiiiiirework!" Taylor sang louder. Jenna and Kenya started singing along—and then Maggie did too. Quiet, shy Maggie. I couldn't help it. I joined in.

When we got out of the van at East Lewiston, we were all cracking up. The players on the East Lewiston team, the Leopards, were warming up on the court, batting the ball back and forth across the net.

I scanned the stands and saw Jim and Blake and waved to them. Then I warmed up with the team. We did stretches, squats, and jumping jacks.

"My face feels like a fiiiiiirework!" Taylor sang out as we exercised, and we all cracked up again.

A few minutes later Coach Patel called us out onto the court. I didn't have time to be nervous. He assigned us positions. I was in position six, between Kenya and Jenna. Summer, Taylor, and Maggie took positions two, three, and four.

We all might have been goofing around a few minutes before, but once the game started, everyone had their game faces on. Kenya sent her first serve to the far left corner, where it soared past the Leopards server and slammed onto the court, scoring the first point of the game. We all cheered.

"Nice one, Kenya!" Taylor yelled.

Her next shot landed in the middle. The Leopards passed it and set it to their front middle hitter, who tried to spike it—but Summer blocked it and nailed it between two players.

We'd scored another point.

My heart started to pound with excitement and I got itchy, waiting for my turn to hit the ball. Kenya's next serve was out of bounds. The Leopards rotated, and their serve came right to me.

I extended my arms and put my right hand over

my left hand, ready to pass the ball. The ball hit my wrists instead of my forearms and went a little wonky—to the side instead of straight ahead. But Kenya got it and set it to Summer, who hit it over the net. The Leopards returned the ball to me again and this time, I managed to hit it pretty much straight up in the air. Jenna ran in front of me and tried to pass it to Maggie, but her pass soared over the net and out of bounds.

"Sorry," I said.

"It's cool," Jenna replied. "We're still up."

The Leopards served again. This ball went from Kenya to Maggie to Summer, who returned the ball hard and fast to the back corner of the court, just in bounds. The Leopards missed the ball and it was our turn to serve. We rotated, and I moved into position five.

I was starting to get into a groove. In the next few rounds of play, I set the ball to Taylor, and she spiked it to score a point. I scored my first point when I blocked a spike from the Leopards. A little bit later Kenya set the ball to me and I spiked it hard over the top.

"Way to bring the heat, Elle!" Summer cheered.

I grinned and wiped the sweat away from my eyes. That had felt great!

Finally, it was my turn to serve. I'd always loved serving in gym class, and I knew I was pretty good at it. But I was a little nervous, because we hadn't had a chance to practice it with the team yet.

I started with my left foot a little bit forward and tossed the ball up with my left hand. Then I hit it overhand with my right hand, aiming it for a gap between the players. One of the players got to it, but she shanked the ball wildly out of the way.

Taylor clapped her hands. "All right! Looks like we got an ace on our team!"

My next serve wasn't as perfect, and we lost control of the ball. But nobody called me out about it. Coach didn't yell. And the next time I got a chance to serve, I made it count. I aimed it for the back of the court, and the Leopard middle blocker thought it was going to go out of bounds. But it landed right on the line. Another point!

The game went by really fast. I can't remember

each and every play, but I do remember that we were all playing our best and having a good time. And in the end we won by five points!

Jim and Blake came onto the court to congratulate me. Blake gave me a high five, and Jim gave me a hug.

"Great job, Elle," Jim said.

"Yeah," Blake said. "You looked great out there—like you actually knew what you were doing."

"Thanks. It was fun," I said, and laughed.

Then Kenya called to me. "Elle! We're hitting the road."

I thanked Jim and Blake for coming and then headed outside with my team.

"We did it!" Jenna cheered as we climbed into the van.

"Elle, you rocked it out," Taylor said. "Awesome."

"Thanks! I loved playing," I said. "You guys are a great team."

"*We're* a great team," Summer said, smiling at me.

And then my stomach growled loudly, and everyone laughed.

"Sorry," I said. "I forgot to eat something before practice today."

"That's why we always go out for pizza after Friday-night games," Kenya said. "Can you come? Sorry, we should have told you."

"I'll text my mom," I said. Luckily, she gave me the okay to go.

After we got back to Spring Meadow, we changed out of our uniforms and then Summer's mom picked us up in her minivan. By the time we got to Sal's Pizzeria, I thought I was going to faint from hunger.

The place was crowded, even though it was almost nine o'clock at night. We lined up to give our orders.

"What can I get for you?" the man behind the counter asked Taylor, who was first in line.

She burst out into song. *"I just want a fiiiiiirework!"*

"Taylor!" Jenna shrieked, and we all started laughing.

The counter guy sighed. I guess he was having a long night.

"Seriously, I'll have a slice of chicken bacon ranch, please," Taylor said.

"Elle, is that you?"

I turned at the sound of the voice behind me—and saw Avery, with Natalie and Hannah. At first I was happy to see them.

"Oh, hey, guys," I said. "We were just, uh, celebrating. We won."

Hannah and Natalie looked at each other.

"That's great," Avery said. "You can sit with us if you want."

At that moment Taylor called out to me. "Hey, Ace! You with us?"

I felt so torn! I wanted to sit with Avery, Hannah, and Natalie. But I also wanted to celebrate with my team.

I turned to Avery. "I'm gonna . . . we won the game, so we're going to celebrate. But good luck with your game on Sunday."

"Will you come see us, *Ace*?" Natalie asked.

"We miss you," Hannah added. "Even though you're not on the team, we still want to hang out. You should come."

That question flustered me. I wanted to support

my friends, but I knew it would be weird to watch them playing without me.

"I, um, I think I have something to do," I said. "With Zobe."

Natalie rolled her eyes. "Whatever."

Whatever. That stung, but I didn't have time to dwell on it. It was time for me to order my pizza.

"I'll text you," I told Avery, and then I moved up to join my team.

Red Light, Green Light

Let's hang out tomorrow? I texted Avery that night, as soon as I got home. I hated the idea that things were getting weird between us. So I checked my schedule and saw that I had some free time on Saturday, along with some home-work time and Zobe time. And I wanted to spend that free time with Avery.

When? she texted back right away.

Around 11? Meet downtown?

👍

I felt relieved as I put the phone down. Avery and

I just needed to hang, and talk, and everything would go back to normal. I was looking forward to seeing her the next morning—but first, I had to bring Zobe to obedience class with Dad.

Zobe is almost three feet tall and weighs 145 pounds. That's about right for a Great Dane, but it's pretty big for a dog. It's one of the reasons I wanted to adopt him. I'm pretty big for a twelve-year-old human, and I used to feel kind of bad about that. Then I saw Zobe at a pet adoption event, and I fell in love.

Zobe is an awesome dog, but he's not perfect. He's got tons of energy and I make sure he gets plenty of exercise, but he still gets really excited when he's around small dogs and small kids. He chases them and that can get messy, like when he knocked into the food table on Thanksgiving.

Dad signed Zobe up for an obedience class on Saturday mornings. I'd gone to the first class, and then Dad agreed I could go to every other one, since my schedule was so busy.

After two classes Zobe could sit, stay, and come on command. Dad had learned this thing called "loose leash walking," which is basically a way to walk your dog so that he doesn't pull you behind him. Dad had showed me, and I'd been trying it out on Zobe. When he pulled, I took a few steps backward and called him to me and gave him a tiny treat. Then we would start walking again. If Zobe pulled again, I would walk backward again—and I kept doing it until Zobe got the idea that it was better to walk alongside me instead of in front of me. It only took a week for him to get the hang of it. But I'm not surprised—he is such a smart dog!

Even so, as soon as we got to the dog training center, Zobe pulled me forward so he could pounce on Bruiser, a little Chihuahua he'd made friends with on his first day of class.

"Yip! Yip! Yip!" Bruiser barked, telling Zobe to bug off. I pulled Zobe away.

"Sit," I told him, and he obeyed, calmly getting into the sit position. Then I turned to Bruiser's owner, a gray-haired lady with glasses. "Hi, Betty."

"Hello, Elle. It's nice to see you here with your father again," she said, with a nod to my dad.

"Zobe's been good about pulling," I said. "But he gets so excited when he sees Bruiser."

Valerie, the trainer, overheard us. "It's really common for dogs to get overexcited, especially energetic dogs like Zobe," she said. "But there's a fix for that. Today we're going to play a fun game of red light, green light that will help our dogs learn impulse control."

"That sounds like fun," Dad said.

At that moment Zobe sprang up and pounced on Bruiser again, completely covering the dog's tiny body with his massive one. Bruiser yipped and did a little dance around his legs. I pulled him away again.

"Oh boy," I said. "I hope this works!"

When class started, Valerie had everyone go around and talk about any issues they'd had with their dog during the week. Then we reviewed sit, stay, and come.

"Now we're going to play red light, green light," Valerie announced. "Everybody, line up against that wall."

There were seven dogs in the class. Dad, Zobe,

and I ended up at the end of the line. Betty and Bruiser were to our right.

"We're going to do this off leash," Valerie began. "When I say, 'Green light!' run across the room with your dog. When I yell, 'Red light!' stop and ask your dog to sit. Once they sit, give them a treat. That's your green light to move again, so say, 'Let's go!' and start running again. Then stop when I say, 'Red light!' Everybody got it?"

"Got it!" I said confidently. I smiled at Dad. This was going to be fun.

"Green light!" Valerie called, and I raced forward with Zobe at my heels.

"Red light!"

I stopped. "Sit, Zobe!"

Zobe skidded to a stop. He circled back and stared at me.

"Sit!" I repeated.

His butt touched the ground and I gave him a tiny treat. "Good boy," I said. "Now let's go!"

We had only gone a few steps when Valerie called out "Red light!" again. This time Zobe came to a stop a little quicker. I repeated with the treat, the praise, and then we turned around and headed back toward Dad.

We stopped two more times on the way back, and by the fourth "Red light!" Zobe was going into a sit position without me even asking him to. I couldn't believe it.

"You try it," I told Dad. "Zobe's doing great."

"I can see that," Dad said, and he ran forward. "Come on, Zobe!"

Dad took Zobe from one end of the room and back, and Zobe sat calmly on every "Red light" command. I was impressed . . . until they came back and Zobe, who was off leash, pounced on Bruiser again.

"Zobe, sit!" I commanded.

To my horror, Zobe started to sit down on top of Bruiser!

"Zobe, no!" I cried, but the little dog managed to scoot out of the way before Zobe landed on him.

Betty laughed. "Zobe may be bigger, but Bruiser is faster," she said. "I think it's very sweet the way they get along. Almost like they're brothers."

"I can't imagine what their parents would look like," Dad joked.

After the game we practiced loose leash walking, and Valerie was very impressed with Zobe's progress. That made me feel proud.

When class was over, Dad dropped me off by the library in downtown Greenmont to meet Avery. There's a small park there with a fountain, and a lot of kids hang out there.

Avery walked up to the car. "My mom's going to give us a ride home, Mr. Deluca," she said.

"Great," Dad said. "See you later, Elle."

Zobe said good-bye to me too. "Woof!"

"Can we go to Suddenly Salad?" Avery asked as Dad drove away. "I'm starving."

I nodded. "Sure."

We walked down the street toward the block of small shops and restaurants. With Christmas a week and a half away, the sidewalks were crowded with shoppers. Green wreaths hung from the posts of the street lights. And all the store windows were decorated for the holidays, with snowflakes, elves, and menorahs.

Suddenly Salad was packed, but we managed to find a small table by the window after we got our food.

"Congratulations on winning yesterday," Avery said.

"Thanks," I replied. And then I blurted out what had been on my mind for days. "Listen, I know it's weird that I'm playing with another team. I still don't know if I made the right choice. But I'm having a good time. And it's only for a few weeks. After that I'll probably leave the team, but I'm not sure."

"How is Coach Patel?" Avery asked. "More chill than Coach Ramirez?"

"*Definitely* more chill," I replied. "The whole team is way more relaxed. But still serious about the game at the same time, if you know what I mean."

Avery nodded. "I do. Bianca is definitely *not* relaxed since you've been gone. She's been acting like a second coach, giving everyone critiques and, like, telling people what to do."

I frowned. "Sorry to hear that."

Avery shrugged. "I'm just glad you're happy, Elle."

"I am," I said. "I mean, I miss you and everybody else on the team—well, everybody except Bianca. But I don't miss the pressure from Coach. And I like having time to do extra stuff, like the Buddy Club."

Avery smiled. "What's that like?"

"It's pretty good so far," I said. "We talked about how reaching out to people who need friends is one way to stop bullying before it starts. It got me thinking about Patrice."

"Patrice?" Avery asked.

"Yeah, I mean, she's on the team, but she isn't close friends with anybody," I said. "Even at lunch, she's really quiet. I was thinking maybe we need to, you know, see if she wants to hang out or something."

"That's a nice idea," Avery said. "Sure, I'd do that."

"Cool," I said. "I'll text her."

I texted Patrice, and then Avery and I got quiet for a little bit, eating our salads. Then Avery said, "Can we stop in Connie's Chocolates after this? I got Hannah for Secret Santa, and you know what a sweet tooth she has."

I'd forgotten about the basketball team tradition of Secret Santa. Everybody picked a random teammate and got them a gift. Then, at the team holiday party, you gave your gift and found out who your Secret Santa was. I got a little pang, knowing I'd miss that this year.

Avery must have seen the look on my face. "Hey, you should come to the party! Everybody would love to see you."

"Everybody?" I asked.

Avery bit her lip. "Well, maybe not Bianca. And I'm not sure about Hannah and Natalie. . . ."

"They've been acting weird around me lately, and even ignoring me," I said. "Are they mad at me?"

Avery shrugged. "I think their feelings are hurt that you're hanging out with the volleyball girls. They feel like you ditched them as friends."

"But that's not true!" I said. "They're still my friends!"

"I know that, but that's just how they feel," Avery said. "They were mad that you didn't sit with us at the pizza place yesterday."

"But my team won the game! That's a tradition. You know that," I said.

"I do," Avery said. "That's why you should come to the party. They miss you."

I shook my head. "But I *shouldn't* go to the party. I'm not a part of the team anymore. I can still be their friend, even if I'm not on the team."

Avery frowned. "I guess," she said. "But will you have time? Maybe you should make plans with them separately."

"I could try to do that," I agreed. I gulped down the last cherry tomato in my bowl. "Come on, let's go to Connie's."

Connie's Chocolates might be the happiest place in the world. A crowd of little kids stood in front of the window, watching a moving display of elves making chocolate bars. One elf stirred a pot of chocolate, another elf put the finished bars on a conveyer belt, and the third took them off the conveyer belt and put them in a little wrapped gift box.

Avery and I stopped and watched.

"They're so cute!" I said, staring at the elves.

"And hypnotic," she added, taking me by the arm.

Inside, chocolate candy filled gleaming glass display cases. Strands of tiny white lights twinkled on the ceiling. One case held chocolates shaped like almost everything you could imagine, from animals to vehicles to people.

"Hannah loves the chocolate-covered peanuts," Avery said.

I walked toward the display case of shaped chocolate. "Maybe I should get something too."

Every year I get something for my sister and brother, my parents, and my grandparents, and I never know what to get! I don't know why'd I'd never thought about getting chocolate before. It's delicious, everybody loves it, and it won't sit on a shelf getting dusty like the World's Greatest Dad statue I'd gotten my father when I was nine.

I stared at the shapes. There were so many! Right away I saw a dog that looked like Zobe, which would be perfect for Beth. A chocolate football for Jim. A chocolate Santa for my dad, who loves Christmas. For mom, a chocolate butterfly, because it was so pretty. And chocolate reindeers for Grandma and Grandpa.

Avery came by while the clerk behind the counter was packing up my chocolates and putting them into boxes.

"Elle! Are you buying the whole store?" she asked.

"I wish I could," I said. "These are awesome gifts."

"I know, they're so cute!" Avery agreed. "Look at that little unicorn. Adorbs!"

Then she got distracted by the stuffed animal display in the center of the room. "Oh, look! I see something for my little cousin!"

She darted away. I leaned in to the counter clerk.

"Can I also get the unicorn, please?" I whispered.

The clerk gave me a funny look, but she picked up the unicorn out of the case and put her in a small white box before Avery returned.

"Do you want anything else?" the clerk asked.

"Um, can I get two chocolate mint patties, please?" I asked.

The clerk moved to the case of assorted chocolates and put two patties in a little bag for me. I was paying for my order when Avery approached me.

"All checked out," she said, holding up her bag.

"Me too," I said, taking the bag from the counter clerk. I reached in, took out the two chocolate mint patties, and handed one to Avery.

"Aw," she said. "Remember the first time we came here, when we were, like, six, and Mom bought these for us?"

"I do," I said.

We both bit into ours at the same time, and the icy cold mint tickled the roof of my mouth.

"Brain freeze!" we said at the same time—just like we had when we were six years old, and every time we'd bitten into a chocolate mint patty since.

We started giggling, and right then I knew that everything was cool with Avery, and always would be.

The rest of the Nighthawks . . . well, I wasn't so sure about that.

Patrice Has a Problem

Zobe, you're not helping," I scolded. I was trying to vacuum the living room, but Zobe kept jumping in front of the vacuum cleaner and barking at it.

"Elle, keep him in your room until you're done!" Dad called from the kitchen.

I turned off the vacuum cleaner and sighed. "Fine. Come on, Zobe."

I ran upstairs and Zobe raced after me, nearly knocking me down. He started whimpering as soon as I closed the door.

"Just a few minutes, I promise!" I told him.

I raced downstairs and finished up vacuuming just as the doorbell rang. I ran to answer it.

"Hey, guys!" I told Avery and Patrice. "Come on in."

"Mmm, something smells good in here," Avery said, sniffing the air. "That has to be your dad's famous spaghetti and meatballs."

"You know it is," I replied. "Dinner's ready in about an hour. Want to hang in my room?"

The day before, Patrice had answered my text and said she was cool with getting together. So I asked Mom if Avery and Patrice could come over for Sunday dinner. Dad cooks up a huge Italian meal every week, and there's always enough for any guests who stop by. I'd wanted to fit in a doggy date with Amanda and Freckles that day too, but Amanda had to go to her grandmother's house after the basketball game that morning.

I'd also meant to make plans with Natalie and Hannah, but that would have to wait. I was glad that

I could finally hang out with Patrice, like I'd been meaning to.

The three of us headed up to my room, and I opened the door, forgetting that Zobe was in there. He bounded out and knocked right into Patrice with his two front paws!

"Zobe, stop! I mean, red light!" I shouted. "I mean, SIT!"

Thankfully, Zobe sat.

"Patrice, meet Zobe," I said.

She scratched the top of his head. "Hey there, boy," she said, and she was smiling, which is not something you usually see Patrice do.

"Come on in," I said.

I grabbed some pillows from my bed and threw them on the floor. I sat down, leaning back against the bed. Avery sat cross-legged on one of the pillows with her back perfectly straight (her mom's a yoga teacher, so she does a lot of yoga), and Patrice picked up a pillow and clutched it to her chest as she sat down. Patrice has black hair that she wears pulled back, even when she's not playing basketball, and really dark, intense eyes.

"So, how was the game today?" I asked.

"We lost," Avery reported. "By six points."

"That's pretty close," I said, but I knew from experience that close wasn't the same as winning.

"I missed an easy layup," Patrice said. "I'm going to hear it from Mom at practice tomorrow."

"It must be hard having your mom as coach," I said.

She nodded. "Yeah, it is. I think she's a lot harder on me than everyone else. I tried to quit that one time but . . . ."

"She wouldn't let you?" Avery asked.

Patrice shook her head. "Nope. I mean, I love basketball, so I didn't really want to quit. It'll be easier when I'm on the high school team. I just have to stick with it."

Then she looked at me. "Why exactly did you quit? I know Mom was tough on you, too. Is that it? Or were you just sick of basketball?"

I couldn't help thinking that Patrice was more talkative than I'd ever known her to be.

"It was a lot of things," I answered her. "I wanted to see what else was out there. I still like basketball. Maybe I even love it. But yeah, your mom being tough on me was part of it. And Bianca didn't help either."

Patrice nodded. "Yeah, I get that."

She shifted position on the floor, and she winced, like she was in pain.

"You okay?" I asked. "Did you hurt yourself on the court?"

"No, it's weird," she said. "I haven't been feeling good since the summer. Like, I get headaches a lot, and I'm tired all the time. And my knees and my elbows hurt for no reason."

Avery frowned. "That sounds serious, Patrice. What does your mom say?"

Patrice bit her lip. "I haven't told her. She'll just think I'm trying to get out of basketball if I do."

"You should talk to her," I said. "I know your mom is a tough coach, but she'd want to know if you're feeling sick."

Patrice sighed. "Yeah, maybe."

"So, hey, what are you doing over the break?" Avery asked, changing the subject. We talked about normal stuff for a while, and then Dad called us down to dinner.

We headed to the dining room, and I introduced Patrice to the rest of the family: Dad, Beth, Jim, and Jim's girlfriend, Alyssa. Dad had made a huge bowl of spaghetti and meatballs, plus garlic bread, salad, and sautéed broccoli rabe. Avery knelt down in front of Beth and let Beth sniff her head. Avery signed "hello" into Beth's hand, and my sister smiled.

"Is that how you say hi?" Patrice asked.

"Beth knows us by our scent," I explained. "Avery's been around for so long that Beth knows hers, too."

"I'd like to say hi," Patrice said in such a simple, sweet way that I wanted to hug her. A lot of people are shy or awkward when they first meet Beth, but not Patrice, and that meant something. I could tell my mom thought so too by the way she was beaming.

"Sure," I said, and I took Patrice by the hand and we went to Beth. I let Beth sniff my head, and then

I signed "friend" into her hand. Then I put Patrice's hand in Beth's. Patrice smiled, and so did my sister.

"All right, everybody," Dad said. "*Mangiamo!*"

Mangiamo means "let's eat" in Italian, and that's what we did. Dinner was delicious, and Patrice was talking with everybody and smiling and laughing the whole time.

Later, after Avery and Patrice left, Mom talked to me.

"That Patrice is such a lovely girl," she said. "I'm glad you invited her over."

"So am I," I said.

I realized that I'd never have invited Patrice over if I hadn't gone to the Buddy Club meeting. And I wouldn't have gone to the Buddy Club if I hadn't quit basketball.

Maybe, I thought, *quitting the team was the right decision after all!*

Eleven Is My Number

"There is nothing fun about *fundamentals*!" Taylor moaned at Tuesday's volleyball practice.

Coach Patel was drilling us on the basics: passing, setting, hitting, and serving. I appreciated it, because all this stuff was new to me. But I could see where it might get repetitive if you did it all the time.

"Mastering the fundamentals is how you will excel," Coach Patel promised.

"I know. I just wish we could play, too," Taylor said, lobbing a pass to me across the court.

I spoke up. "Would it be weird to have a three-on-three scrimmage game?" I asked.

"I've thought about it, but I don't know if it would work," Coach replied. "You'd have to do a lot of running around to cover the court."

"We should try it," Taylor urged him.

"Yeah, why not?" Summer asked.

"Okay, then," Coach said. He looked at us. "Kenya, Maggie, Elle on one side. Taylor, Summer, and Jenna on the other. One of you from each side, play the net."

"Hooray!" Taylor cheered, and we all quickly ran into place.

Taylor served the ball over the net, and I had to run to the corner to get to it. I passed to Maggie, who set to Kenya. She had to run back from the net to get the ball, so she couldn't spike it over. But she hit with all her might, and Jenna and Summer had to scramble.

It was a pretty crazy practice game! We all spent twice as much energy as usual, chasing after the ball. But we all got to scrimmage—setting, hitting, and serving in a game setting—which was a lot more fun than just doing drills.

I liked getting to run around the court more instead of standing in basically the same place when the ball was in play. As much as I was learning to love volleyball, I really missed that free feeling of tearing down the court.

When practice ended, we were all sweaty messes.

Taylor punched me on the shoulder. "Great idea, Ace! What did we ever do without you?"

I think I blushed. It was really flattering to be given such a cool nickname after only one week of playing. In basketball the only nickname I'd earned was Runaway Train, for going out of bounds. Ace was a lot better.

Still, things kept happening that made me miss basketball. On Thursday I volunteered at Camp Cooperation, an after-school program for kids with special needs. Inside the multipurpose room the kids were gathered around tables with Brian, Janette, and Vicky—the adults who ran the program. A blond-haired boy with Down syndrome—Pete, my friend Caroline's little brother—ran up to me.

"Elle! We can't go outside today!" Pete said.

"I know, Pete," I said. "But we can have fun inside."

"We're making snowmen," he said, pointing to a bowl of white foam balls on the table. "It's boring."

"I don't know. I think it looks fun," I said. "Come on, I'll help you."

I led Pete back to the table and sat down next to him and his friend Max, who was quietly coloring a picture of a reindeer.

I reached for one of the white foam balls. "This looks like a good one for the bottom," I said. "What do you think?"

"You don't play basketball anymore," Pete blurted out.

It was the first time I'd seen Pete since I'd quit. I should have known he would have something to say about it. When I played, he was my biggest cheerleader.

"No, I don't," I said.

"But you were the best player," Pete said.

"There are lots of good players on the team," I said. "Anyway, I'm playing volleyball now."

"That's when you hit the ball over the net," Pete stated.

I nodded. "Yes."

"Boring," he said, and then he started making a snowman, so I guess he thought that volleyball was even more boring than doing crafts!

Then Patrice walked in and removed her soaking-wet rain jacket. A freezing, early winter rain had been falling all day.

"Sorry I'm late," she said. "I was in the nurse's office with a really bad headache. But it's better now."

Another headache, I thought. It didn't sound like Patrice had talked to her mom about how she was feeling.

Patrice must have caught the look on my face. "Really, I'm okay," she said.

"Patrice, come make a snowman!" Pete called out, and Patrice smiled and sat down at the table with us. We had fun, and by the time camp was over, I'd forgotten to be worried about her.

• • •

"Two is her number!" Kenya yelled.

"Two is her number!" the rest of the volleyball team shouted back.

"Maggie is her name!" Kenya yelled.

"Maggie is her name!" we repeated.

"She's one reason!"

"She's one reason!"

"We're gonna win the game!" Kenya finished.

Then Kenya moved on to the next player.

"Three is her number!"

We kept the chant going until we'd cheered for every member of the team. I have to admit, I got a little thrill when I heard my name and my number— eleven. When we finished, we started clapping and cheering.

We were in the Spring Meadow middle school gym, ready to face a club team from Wilmington. They were undefeated, and I knew Kenya was trying to get us psyched up in the face of certain defeat.

I was excited to play in another game, to see what would happen. And I was even more excited when I saw some familiar faces in the stands: Amanda and Caroline, who had brought Pete with her.

Pete waved at me. "Go Elle! Play boring volleyball!"

Caroline nudged him, but I laughed. It was really sweet that they had come to the game. I waved at Amanda, and she waved back.

Then it was time for the game. Coach had put me in position four, up by the net. I got a good look at the Wilmington team. They had a lot of players on the bench, which meant that they wouldn't get tired out as quickly as we would. This wasn't going to be easy, but I wasn't nervous. I knew we were all going to play our best. And have fun doing it.

Wilmington served. The ball flew to Kenya, who was in the serving position, deep in the corner. She had to lunge for it, and when she made contact, the ball shot between Taylor and Jenna and they both missed it.

Wilmington started clapping in rhythm. "You better duck, you better hide, 'cause Ava's serving to your side!" they chanted.

Taylor turned to me and rolled her eyes. Ava served again for Wilmington. She aimed it in the same place, but this time, Kenya was ready for it. She passed it nicely to Summer, who set me up at the front of the net, and I spiked it over, past Wilmington's blockers and defense. We'd won the serve!

Taylor high-fived me, and my energy was pumping. With that one rally, we'd proven that we had what it took to beat Wilmington. And that's exactly what we did.

It was a close game, and it wasn't easy. They scored a few points by spiking the ball over the net, but whenever I was blocking I made sure they never got past me. That was a good feeling. And I was getting a lot better at setting the ball. I set one to Maggie that she bounced between two of the Wilmington players!

In the end we won by two points. We formed a circle, jumping up and down and hugging one another. Then we shook hands with the Wilmington team.

Amanda, Caroline, and Pete came down from the stands.

"What do you think, Pete?" I asked. "Was it boring?"

"Only kind of boring," Pete said. "You were the best, Elle."

I shook my head. "I really need to make you my official personal cheerleader," I said.

"Well, he's right," Amanda said. "It's so not fair. You're great at basketball, and you're great at volleyball, too."

"I'm just having fun," I said.

"And you're winning," Caroline pointed out.

I glanced over at my team. "Well, I should go get changed."

"Can you come to the Nighthawks game tomorrow?" Amanda asked.

I really wanted to say yes. But I still couldn't face the idea of watching them play without me.

"Maybe," I said. Then I lied. "I think we might be doing some family holiday thing."

"Okay. Maybe I'll see you over break?" she asked.

"Definitely," I said.

I turned to Caroline and Pete. "If I don't see you guys, have a Merry Christmas."

"Merry Christmas, Elle!" Pete said.

I ran to meet up with my team for some postgame pizza, and I felt light. We'd won our game, my friends had come to see me, and I had a whole week off from school and volleyball to look forward to.

It kind of surprised me, but I realized that I felt happier than I had in a long time!

Jingle All the Way

*W*ake up, Elle! It's Christmas! Wake up, Elle! Wake up! Zobe pleaded.

Actually, I could only *hear* Zobe talking to me in my dream state. But that's what he might as well have been saying, because he was licking my face and pawing me, desperately trying to wake me up.

I picked up my phone. 6:30 a.m.!

"Really, Zobe?" I asked.

A few years ago I would have jumped out of bed at 6:30 on Christmas morning. But last night we'd had a big dinner with Grandma and Grandpa, and then gone to midnight mass, and all I wanted to do was sleep.

Obviously, Zobe had other ideas.

I sat up, getting my bearings. When Grandma and Grandpa sleep over, they take my bedroom and Zobe and I camp out in the family room in the basement. I'd brought down some clothes with me, and I quickly got changed into sweatpants and a hoodie, pulled back my hair into a ponytail, and jogged upstairs with Zobe at my heels.

It was quiet upstairs—I was the only one awake. In the living room the white lights of the Christmas tree twinkled on the piles of wrapped presents underneath the tree. I fed Zobe and then put on my sneakers and ran around with him for a while in the backyard. The chilly morning air woke me up, and when I got inside, Grandma was downstairs making coffee. Her short blond hair was messy from sleeping, and she wore red leggings and a red sweatshirt with a Christmas teddy bear on it.

"Merry Christmas, Elle!" she said cheerfully.

I hugged her. "Merry Christmas, Grandma."

"Are you going to wake up your parents and

make them open presents?" she asked.

I laughed. "I'm not eight anymore, Grandma," I said. Then I yawned. "I'm only up this early because of Zobe."

Zobe walked over to Grandma, who patted his head. "He seems much calmer now, Elle."

I nodded. "I think the obedience classes are helping."

Then I heard stomping on the stairs, and Jim bounded into the kitchen.

"Merry Christmas!" he shouted.

I put my hands over my ears. "Seriously, Jim? Aren't you an adult now?"

"It's my last Christmas at home!" he said.

"No, it's not," I said. "You'll be coming home from college next year for Christmas."

"Well, you know what I mean," he said. "I'm just excited, I guess."

Grandma shook her head. "Just like your father," she said. "The Delucas have Christmas in their blood."

"And marinara sauce," Dad added, walking into the kitchen. "I need to get my lasagna started."

"Can we open presents now?" Jim asked.

"Not until Uncle Danny and Aunt Jess get here with the kids," Dad said.

"Aw, come on," Jim pleaded.

I laughed. "Jimmy wants to open up his presents," I teased.

"Don't make fun of me. I got you something awesome," he said.

"Well, I got you something awesome too," I shot back.

"You mean like that flashlight pen you got me last year?" Jim asked.

"Hey, I thought it was useful," I said. "If you didn't like it, I'll take it back!"

I chased after him, and he ran away from me. Zobe raced after both of us, barking.

Mom wheeled Beth into the kitchen, shaking her head. "What is going on in here?"

"Merry Christmas!" I said, crushing her in a hug. Then I knelt down and said good morning to Beth.

"Can you keep it quiet down there?" Grandpa called from upstairs. "It's still the middle of the night!"

"Oh, don't be a scrooge!" Grandma yelled back.

Dad nodded to Jim. "If you make us pancakes, I'll let everyone open one present after breakfast."

Jim made a fist pump. "Yes! Pancakes coming up!"

So we ate pancakes, and each opened one present (mine was a WNBA T-shirt from Dad), and then we helped Mom and Dad get ready for Christmas dinner. By the time Uncle Danny rang the doorbell, the dining room table was set and the house smelled like Dad's lasagna.

Uncle Danny had a pan of chicken parm, and Aunt Jess held bags of presents. My little twin cousins, Michael and Olivia, ran past her.

"Where's Zobe? Where's Zobe?" they chanted.

"We might be able to let Zobe hang up here with us if we're all calm," I told them. "If not, he'll have to go downstairs."

"We'll be calm," Olivia promised, with a very serious look on her face.

I kept an eye on my cousins as they pet Zobe, but once present-opening time came around, they completely ignored him. I had to admit I was starting to feel excited too, even though I knew what to expect.

Grandma always gave me really girly clothes, even though she's never seen me wear them. This year was no different. I pulled a flowery skirt and a blouse with ruffles out of the gift bag.

"Thanks, Grandma," I said. I held the skirt up to me, and it was so short—way above my knees! That's usually what happened when Grandma gave me clothes, but she meant well.

I looked at Mom and she nodded, and I knew I'd do what I did every year—I'd give them to Avery. She likes flowers and ruffles just fine.

Uncle Danny and Aunt Jess gave me basketball shoes, like they do every year. I opened the box, hoping maybe they'd done something different this time, knowing I'd quit the team. But inside were a super-sweet pair of black basketball shoes with green stripes. I had begged Mom to get them for me for months, when I was still playing basketball.

"We know you quit the team, Elle," Aunt Jess said apologetically. "But we figured you still like playing for fun, right?"

I thought about that. I don't think I had even

played a game of pickup since I'd joined volleyball. But I nodded. "Sure."

"Besides, you might change your mind," Uncle Danny said. "I mean, somebody with your talent and your height shouldn't throw away a basketball career, Elle."

I felt my face get hot. That expectation of me—that I was destined to play basketball just because I was tall and good at it—wasn't gone now that I'd quit.

"Well, I really like being on the volleyball team," I said.

Uncle Danny shook his head. "Come on, Elle. I mean, volleyball? Basketball's a more serious sport, don't you think?"

"Danny," Dad said in a warning tone.

"I don't know. Volleyball takes a lot of training," I said. And I'm learning how to play all the different positions."

"But it's not basketball," Uncle Danny said.

Aunt Jess put a hand on his arm. "Elle should do whatever makes her happy, Danny," she said, and she smiled at me. "I hope you like the shoes."

"I *love* them!" I said, which was true. They were some of the coolest basketball shoes out there. I gave her a hug, and Uncle Danny, too, even though I was kind of mad at him for getting on my case about not playing basketball.

Then I went upstairs and got down my gifts for everyone—I'd kept my presents in my closet, not under the tree, so Zobe wouldn't eat them.

I handed out the presents I'd gotten them, eager to see their reactions.

"This is too pretty to eat!" Mom exclaimed, holding up her chocolate butterfly.

Jim grinned when he saw his chocolate football. "Awesome. Much better than a flashlight pen. Thanks, Elle."

I stuck my tongue out at him.

"Elle, why don't you take Zobe for a walk before dinner?" Mom suggested.

I jumped up from the living room floor. "Sure!"

Soon Zobe and I were outside, making our way to the park near our house. I glanced at Amanda's yellow house, which was right across the street from the park. The lights were on inside, and I saw some people gathered around her Christmas tree, but I didn't see her. That bummed me out a little bit. I was hoping to run into her.

"Jingle Elle, jingle Elle, jingle all the way . . ."

I heard singing behind me and turned to see Amanda, wearing a silly elf hat, walking her dog, Freckles.

"Jingle Elle?" I groaned.

"Well, I saw you there, and then it struck me that your name rhymes with 'bell,'" she said. "And lots of Christmas songs have bells in the name."

"Oh no," I groaned. I knew what was coming.

"Silver Elle," Amanda sang, *"silver Elle! It's Christmas time in the park. . . ."*

"Stop it!" I cried, giggling.

"I can't help it!" she said. "My family's been singing Christmas carols for the last three hours. That's what happens when your dad plays the piano."

"That sounds like fun," I said.

"So, Merry Christmas," she said. "Taking a Zobe break?"

I nodded. "There's no such thing as a day off when you have a Great Dane."

"That goes for any dog, I think," she said.

Freckles was sniffing Zobe's legs while Zobe patiently stood there.

"Good dog, Zobe," I said.

"He is a good dog," Amanda said. "I'm glad you got him, so we have dogs to walk together."

"Yeah, it's cool," I agreed.

"I should go back home," Amanda said. "Dad needs a soprano for 'O Holy Night.'"

I wasn't exactly sure what she meant by that, but I wanted to find out.

"Cool," I said. "Let's definitely set up an official doggy date before the break is over."

She smiled. "Sure. I'll text you later. Bye, Silver Elle!"

"Bye," I said, and I smiled all the way home.

Running into Amanda was a pretty nice present on Christmas Day, I thought. *Even nicer than fancy basketball shoes!*

Awkward!

Adventure League II! 7 p.m. tomorrow at the mall. Who's in?

The text popped up on my phone, and I saw it was a group text from Caroline to our lunch table crew, and Amanda.

So in!! Avery replied.

Me too! I chimed in. The first *Adventure League* movie had been awesome, about a group of female professional athletes who searched for treasure in dangerous places when they were in the off-season. I knew I was going to love the second one.

Amanda replied next. ☹ **Sorry, I gotta go to my aunt's.**

Then Patrice. **Mom says I can go!**

Finally, Natalie and Hannah weighed in.

Can't make it! Natalie texted.

Me neither, Hannah added.

I thought it was cool that Caroline was organizing a movie for all of us, and except for being sorry that Amanda couldn't make it, I didn't really notice exactly who was going and who wasn't. It was still holiday break, and I knew a lot of people weren't around.

The morning of the movie Caroline sent a text saying we were going to the movie theater in town instead of the one at the mall. No big deal. But it led to kind of a big problem.

When Mom dropped me off at the theater, I found Caroline and Patrice right away.

It's awesome that Patrice is here, I thought. *I think this is the first time she's ever gone out with any of us, except that time she came to my house for dinner!*

Avery arrived at the same time as I did.

"Are we waiting for anybody else?" she asked.

"Just us," Caroline said. "Come on, let's get tickets."

We got our tickets and then headed into the crowded theater lobby.

"Snack bar!" Avery called out. "I can't watch a movie without popcorn."

"Even after dinner?" Patrice asked.

"I saved room," Avery said. "I'll get a big one and we can share it."

"Thanks, Avery," Caroline said. "I'll share my candy with you."

I bought a bottle of water and the four of us followed Avery over to the stand where you butter your popcorn. We passed by the soda dispensing machines, and I spotted a head of pink hair from the corner of my eye.

Natalie, Hannah, and Bianca were all filling up cups of soda and laughing. That's when it registered: Natalie and Hannah had said they couldn't come to the movies with us. And here they were with Bianca.

Behind me, Avery spoke up. "Hey, guys. Thought you couldn't go to the movies with us?"

Hannah froze and looked at Natalie. Then it dawned on me: They'd thought we would be at the mall theater. Had they come to the one in town just to avoid us?

"Well, our plans changed," Natalie said. "Anyway, we're not even going to see *Adventure League II*. We thought the first one was kind of lame."

"You should have told us," Avery pressed them. "We would have picked another movie."

Natalie shrugged. "Whatever."

"Enjoy your movie!" Bianca called out cheerfully. But boy, was the air thick with awkwardness!

"Come on, our movie's starting," I said, and I, Avery, Caroline, and Patrice walked away.

Avery was furious. "You know, I told those two they needed to get over it, Elle, or you'd never come back!"

I stopped. "What do you mean?"

"I just mean they've both had an attitude since you left the team," Avery said. "You said so yourself. So I talked to them and said they should be nicer to you, or you'd never come back to the team."

"They were never the real problem," I reminded

her. "It was Coach. And Bianca. And what made you think I would even come back?"

"Well, you said so yourself that volleyball is only temporary," Avery said. "I guess I thought maybe you'd think about rejoining the team. There's still time before the season ends."

My mind was spinning. "I don't know what I'm going to do when Lauren's wrist gets better," I said. "I might just go back to having extra free time. I might stick with the volleyball team. I mean, I don't even know if I'll ever play basketball again."

A worried look crossed Avery's face. "I know," she said. "Listen, we don't have to talk about this now. Let's go see the movie."

I was freaking out a little bit inside. It seemed like Hannah and Natalie didn't even want to be my friends anymore. And it was so weird that they were hanging out with Bianca. I didn't even think they really liked her!

But what freaked me out even more was Avery's remark that she thought I would come back to the basketball team. I mean, I'd never said I was giving up on basketball forever. But she seemed to think I would go back to it right away, and that's not something I was sure I wanted to do.

Luckily, I stopped freaking out when the movie started. It was just as awesome as I hoped it would be. My favorite character had always been Athena, the professional basketball player, but when I watched the film this time, I paid attention to Julie, the Olympic volleyball player. She was pretty cool and had some awesome volleyball skills that I wished I had too. I made a note to watch the US women's team from the last Olympics if I could find it on the Internet when I got home.

It was almost 9:30 when the movie ended and the credits rolled. We all got up—except for Patrice. I looked down and saw that she was sleeping!

I gently nudged her. "Patrice! You okay?"

She woke up and yawned. "Oh yeah, sorry. Just really tired."

"Is it part of what you told me?" I asked quietly. "Headaches, feeling tired, hurting knees, stuff like that?"

She nodded.

"Did you tell your mom?" Avery asked.

Patrice shook her head. "Not yet. I'm still worried she's just going to think I'm faking."

It bugged me that Patrice hadn't told her mom. So when my mom picked me up from the mall, I decided to tell her.

"How was the movie?" Mom asked.

"Really good," I replied. "It was a little weird in the beginning, though, because Hannah and Natalie came to see another movie, after they told us they couldn't come with us. I think they're avoiding me."

Mom sighed. "Friendships can be difficult at your age, Elle. You and your friends are still figuring out who you are and the kind of people you want to be with."

"They think I ditched them as friends for my volleyball friends," I said. "But that's not true. They'll always be my friends, no matter what team I'm on."

"Have you told them that?" Mom asked.

I had to think about that. "No, not exactly. Avery talked to them."

"Maybe you should be the one to do that," Mom said.

I nodded. "Yeah, maybe you're right," I said. Then I brought up Patrice. "So, Patrice hasn't been feeling well. But she doesn't want to tell her mom, because she thinks her mom will think she's faking it to get out of basketball."

Mom raised her eyebrows. "I'm sure Coach Ramirez would want to know if something is wrong with her daughter. How is Patrice feeling?"

"She gets headaches a lot," I reported. "And she feels tired all the time. She even fell asleep during the movie."

"My goodness!" Mom said.

"Oh, and she says stuff hurts her, like her knees and elbows," I said.

Mom frowned. "This sounds an awful lot like Lyme disease."

"I've heard of that," I said. "You get it from ticks, right?"

She nodded. "Yes, it's caused by bacteria transmitted through the bite of a tick," she said. "It can be serious, but it's manageable. I'm going to give Coach Ramirez a call and talk to her about it."

"Thanks," I said. "I was getting worried about her."

"I hope you'll always come to me when you're worried about something," Mom said, and I reached over and squeezed her arm. How cool was it to have a Mom I could talk to about stuff? I don't think I'd ever been too scared to talk to her about anything—and only now did I realize how lucky I was.

"Love you," I said.

"Love you too, Elle."

A Fresh Start

appy New Year!" Avery greeted us at the front door.

"Thanks, Avery," Dad said. "Only four hours and forty-seven minutes left to go!"

Mom, Dad, and I walked inside Avery's house, which was filled with her neighbors. Grown-ups gathered around the dining room table, which was piled with food, and little kids chased one another around the living room. On the TV, people wearing coats, scarves, and hats gathered outside in New York City to watch musicians perform and a giant glittery ball drop in Times Square.

Avery hugged me. "I'm so glad you made it!"

"Me too," I replied. Avery's family had invited us to their New Year's party every year, but we usually stayed home with Beth. Beth always fell asleep before midnight, so we did too.

This year Beth's babysitter offered to stay with her, so we ordered in Chinese food and all had dinner together. Then Jim and his girlfriend Alyssa headed out to a party and we drove to Pine Creek, where Avery's family lives. (That was one of the things about going to a private school in Wilmington. The students there lived in all different towns. Sometimes I wished Avery lived next door, like Blake did!)

"My goodness, Avery, you look lovely!" Mom said.

Avery's dark brown hair flowed down her back in loose curls, and she wore a silvery dress with silver ballet flats to match. I had gotten dressed for the party in my nicest jeans and the WNBA T-shirt Dad had given me for Christmas.

"Thanks," Avery said, and then she grabbed

my arm. "Come on, Elle, you've got to try Dad's brownies before they're all gone."

Avery's house is usually very peaceful and calm, because Avery is an only child, but also because her mom is the chillest person I've ever met. But tonight the house was bananas. Avery and I had to push our way to the food table. It was loaded with food that her parents had made and her neighbors had brought: grapes, cheese, hummus, mini pizzas, cookies, brownies, tiny hot dogs, and more. If my belly hadn't been full of pork lo mein and dumplings I would have tasted everything. But I did have room for one of Mr. Morgan's brownies.

We grabbed the brownies and made our way to a corner of the room. Avery's mom approached us, holding a metal bowl with little pieces of paper and pencils in it.

"Elle! Happy New Year!" she said, giving me a hug. She looked as festive as Avery, but in a different way. She wore a purple flowy dress and a bunch of colorful beaded necklaces. She had the same friendly brown eyes that Avery did.

She handed me paper and a pencil.

"What's this for?" I asked.

"Some people make resolutions on New Year's Eve," she replied. "But in this house we also get rid of what we don't want in our lives any more. Write down something you want to get rid of and throw it in the firepit outside when you're done."

Somebody called her name then, and she left. I looked at Avery. "I'm not sure what to write."

"Let's go where it's quiet," she said, and she led me to a small room off the dining room—the Morgans' meditation room—where we sat down on some cushions on the floor.

I felt myself let out a breath. "I love it in here," I said.

"It's a good place to think," Avery agreed.

"So, what did you write?" I asked her.

"Well . . . ," she began slowly. "I wrote that I wanted to stop being insecure about the way I look."

My eyebrows shot up. "But Avery, you're gorgeous! What are you talking about?"

"I am *not* social media gorgeous," she shot back.

"I have super bushy eyebrows and I'm starting to break out all the time."

"All those people on social media are using filters," I argued. "Nobody looks like that in real life."

Avery sighed. "I know," she said. "But it doesn't feel like that, most of the time. That's why I added it to the firepit. See how that works?"

I nodded. "I get it," I said. I quickly wrote down: *Stop feeling bad about my height.*

That wasn't going to be easy, I knew. But it was getting easier. Adopting Zobe had helped.

"Can I see?" she asked, and I nodded. She looked over my shoulder and I showed her. "Good one," she said. "Anything else?"

I closed my eyes and thought. Then I opened them and wrote: *Stop feeling guilty about quitting basketball.*

"You still feel guilty?" Avery asked.

"I do," I said. "Like at the movies the other day, when you said you were still hoping I'd come back to the team."

"Well, I'm allowed to hope that," Avery said.

"But just because I do doesn't mean you have to feel guilty. Does that make sense?"

I nodded. "I guess so."

"So, do you think you *might* come back?" she asked.

"I honestly don't know!" I replied. "Every time I think about it, I remember how miserable I was all the time."

She frowned. "I didn't realize you were miserable. That's pretty serious."

"Well, I was," I said. "There was so much pressure! I don't feel that kind of pressure on the volleyball team. It's a lot more fun."

"Maybe there's not as much pressure because you're only filling in for Lauren," Avery suggested.

I nodded. "That could be. But also, Coach Patel is a lot nicer than Coach Ramirez. And nobody calls me names or gives me a hard time, like Bianca does."

"That's fair," Avery agreed. "But didn't you have any fun at all playing basketball?"

I thought about it. "I guess I did," I said. "I mean, I love all my friends on the team. But then the bad stuff got worse than the good stuff."

"When you said you might never play basketball again, that kind of freaked me out," Avery told me. "I mean, that's a big thing to say."

I sighed. "I know. I don't think I meant it. I do think about playing again someday. But just not now."

I wrote again on my paper. *Stop being so indecisive!*

"Anything else you want to write down?" Avery asked.

I thought about it. "I want to fix things with Hannah and Natalie. I still haven't done that."

"So maybe say something like, 'No more problems with Hannah and Natalie,'" Avery suggested.

"That sounds good," I agreed, and I added one last statement to my paper.

Avery jumped to her feet. "To the fire!" she said.

"To the fire!" I echoed.

We headed out to her backyard, where a bunch of people were gathered around the firepit, including both our dads. I folded my paper in half and then in half again, so nobody would see what was written on it.

"Do I have to say anything?" I asked Avery.

She shook her head. "Nope. Unless you want to."

I tossed the paper into the flames. *Good-bye!* I thought.

This may sound weird, but as I watched the paper burn, I felt better. Lighter, somehow. And excited for the new year to start.

Avery looked at her phone. "Three and a half hours until midnight," she said with a sigh. "It always seems to take forever for midnight to come, every year. What should we do?"

I glanced over at the basketball hoop hanging from her garage and wiggled my eyebrows. Avery grinned.

"Let me change into my sneakers!"

"And let's put jackets on," I added. "It's chilly out!"

A few minutes later we were shooting hoops in the driveway. As we played, more people came to join us: my dad, some of Avery's neighbors, and a couple of kids. Soon we had a decent game of pickup going.

Before we knew it, Avery's mom called to everybody outside.

"Come on in, everyone! It's almost midnight!"

Avery and I looked at each other. I knew I had sweat stains under my armpits. Avery's hair was plastered against her face. We laughed.

I realized that I'd had more fun playing basketball that night than I had in a long time. That meant something. It meant I *could* have fun playing basketball. And that I still liked it.

We went inside to watch the giant ball drop. We drank sparkling apple cider from plastic champagne glasses, and Dad made Avery and me each eat twelve grapes at midnight, because that's supposed to be good luck in Italy. Then it was time to go, and Avery and I hugged.

"Best New Year's ever?" she asked.

I nodded. "Definitely," I agreed.

I couldn't wait to see what the new year would bring . . . and if basketball would be a part of it.

Cheers to Friendship

We went back to school a couple of days later, on Thursday. It was kind of weird going back with only two days left in the week, and everybody was yawning and out of it.

Except for Patrice. She met me at my locker that morning, and she was smiling and happy.

"Hey, Elle," she said. "How was your New Year's?"

"Nice," I said. "How about yours?"

"I just wanted to thank you," she said. "Your mom talked to my mom."

"I hope you don't mind," I said. "But I was worried about you."

She nodded. "It's okay. My mom wasn't mad at me at all. She took me for some tests and it turns out your mom was right. I have Lyme disease."

"Oh no!" I cried.

"Yeah, it stinks," she said. "I probably got it at basketball camp over the summer. We went for a hike in the woods one day and I didn't use the bug spray because I didn't like how it smelled."

I wrinkled my nose. "Yeah, bug spray smells awful."

"But it might have saved me from a tick bite," Patrice said. "Anyway, that's just the bad news. The good news is that now I can get it treated. The medication will help me feel better. And maybe play better too."

"That is good news," I said. "I'm glad you figured it out."

"It's all because of you, Elle," Patrice said. "My mom and I had a really good talk. I was nervous about telling her I wasn't feeling good, and I shouldn't have been. She was so understanding about everything!"

"That's good," I said.

"We even talked about how she pushes me so hard on the team," Patrice went on. "She said she tries to separate being a mom and my coach. But she admitted that she might be taking things too far."

She paused and looked at me. "Maybe you can talk to her too, Elle. I know she's one reason why you left the team."

"I tried talking to her once before," I said. "It didn't really help."

"Just think about it," Patrice said, and I told her I would.

I was happy that Patrice was going to be feeling better soon, and that mood lasted all morning. Because we were just back from break, the teachers took it easy on us too. Ms. Ebear had us watch a video about African history. In gym Mr. Patel didn't make us do squats and push-ups, like he usually does. Everyone seemed a lot more relaxed than usual.

Then I went to lunch, and tensed up a little as

I walked into the cafeteria. I was ready to tackle something I'd been meaning to do for a few days: talk to Natalie and Hannah.

I waited until everybody was sitting down and eating lunch. Then I nodded across the table to them.

"So, can we talk?" I asked.

Hannah looked at Natalie. Natalie shrugged. "Sure."

I took a deep breath. "Listen, I just want you to know that you guys are important to me," I said. "I know we haven't been hanging out as much since I quit the team. But I'm still your friend."

"Well, you're not acting like it," Natalie said. "You're hanging out with the volleyball girls."

"We miss you, Elle," Hannah said.

"And you haven't even come to any of our games," Natalie added.

"I know," I said. "I just thought it would feel weird if I went."

"It's weird that you're not on the team," Hannah said. "It's just not the same without you. Is there any chance at all that you might come back?"

"I don't know," I said. "As long as Coach is tough on me, and Bianca keeps giving me a hard time . . . I just don't think I can do it."

Natalie frowned. "Let me talk to Bianca about it," she said. "I know she wants you back on the team."

I glanced over at Bianca's table. "You think that would help?"

"Yeah, she wants to win, and we're a better team with you," Natalie said. "That's just a fact."

"We'll talk to her," Hannah promised.

I thought about this. If Bianca could just get off my back, it would make a big difference. She wasn't the only reason I'd quit the team, though. Maybe it sounds corny, but by joining the Buddy Club and helping out the volleyball team, I was learning some new things about myself. And that felt pretty great.

"I miss you guys too," I said. "Whether I get back on the team or not, I promise we'll hang out more."

"And you'll come see us play?" Hannah asked.

I nodded. "Do you have a game this weekend?" I asked.

Natalie nodded. "Sunday. Home game."

"Then I'll be there," I said. "I promise."

Hannah smiled.

"Are we cool?" I asked.

"Definitely," Natalie said. She ran around the table and hugged me. "Sorry, Elle. I guess we just thought we were losing you as a friend."

Avery held up her metal water bottle. "Cheers to friendship!"

Everyone at the table—me, Avery, Patrice, Caroline, Natalie, and Hannah—grabbed their drink containers and touched them together. Then Caroline asked if anyone had studied for the science quiz yet and we had a nice, normal lunch with no eye rolling or anybody ignoring anybody else.

I was glad I'd taken Mom's advice and talked it out with Natalie and Hannah. The idea of going to a Nighthawks game still made me feel a little bit nervous. But if it meant making my friends happy, I would do it!

The next day was Friday, and we had volleyball practice right after school, even though we didn't have a game that night because of the holidays. Coach Patel had us drill passing. I paired up with Maggie and we passed the ball back and forth. Back and forth. Back and forth . . .

Then we did serving drills. I was still trying to work on my control, so I liked doing that. Then we had another three-on-three practice game.

Besides serving, I think I liked blocking best. It reminded me the most of basketball. Playing that pickup game on New Year's Eve had got me thinking more about what I missed about basketball. Like the adrenaline rush of charging down the court. Or guarding someone coming right at you. In volleyball, being up at the net and staring down the player in front of me was the closest I got to that feeling.

Even though we didn't have a game, we had planned to go out to dinner after practice. Maggie's mom drove us this time, and dropped us off at Burger Shack. When we got there, a girl with curly red hair and a bandage around her wrist was waiting for us—Lauren.

Summer ran and hugged her. "Lauren!"

"Kenya told me you guys were coming here, so I wanted to surprise everybody," she said. "I have good news. The doctor says I can play again in two weeks."

The other girls started talking all at once as we took our seats at a big round table.

"That is awesome!" Maggie said.

"Yeah, that's great news!" Taylor added.

"So, I guess next week will be my last game," I said.

Kenya turned to me. "It doesn't have to be. It would be great to have an extra player. Then we'd be able to sub out once in awhile."

"You don't have to go, Ace," Taylor said.

This kind of took me by surprise. I thought my time on the volleyball team was going to be temporary. Did I want to stay on the team? I wasn't really sure.

"Can I take your order?" the server asked us.

I ordered the ranch burger. *At least that decision was easy*, I thought.

The subject changed to the school's winter ski

trip coming up. A few minutes later the server came to our table with a tray of drinks. His shoe skidded a little on the floor and he lost his balance—but he caught himself just in time. Not a drop spilled.

"Serve it! Serve it! Do not swerve it!" Taylor chanted.

The server smiled. "Volleyball team?" he asked.

"Spring Meadow," Kenya answered.

"Nice," he said. "I'll be looking out for you guys in the 2028 Olympics."

He gave us our drinks and then walked away.

"He was cute," Summer whispered.

Then everyone started talking about cute boys at the school, and I tuned out. I imagined playing volleyball in the 2028 Olympics, in front of a cheering crowd. The ball came flying over the net. I passed it perfectly to Kenya, who set it to Summer, who spiked it over the net for a point.

Pass, set, hit. Pass, set, hit. That was the rhythm of volleyball—so different from the rhythm of basketball. The scene in my head changed to a WNBA game. I tipped off the ball at the start of the game to Avery. Then I tore down the court, avoiding my defenders as Avery dribbled toward the basket. I found an opening and she passed it to me. My defender tried to guard me, but I jumped up high, so high, and tossed the ball into the basket. Two points!

I was starting to realize something. I liked the laid-back vibe of this volleyball team. On the volleyball court I could relax and do my best without worrying about what the expectation of my best was supposed to be. But I missed the action and the moves of playing basketball. If I could have more fun playing basketball, I might be willing to join the team again.

Fun. Why wasn't playing on the Nighthawks fun? I wondered. Was it all the fault of Bianca and Coach Ramirez? Or was the problem inside my own head? I was blaming Coach for putting pressure on me, but was I the one putting pressure on myself?

"Hey, Elle, did you order the ranch burger?" Taylor asked.

I snapped out of my daydream. "Uh, yeah, that's me," I said.

"First one to finish wins!" Taylor cried, taking a monster bite out of her burger.

"Ew, gross!" Summer shrieked.

"Taylor, you should enter one of those eating competitions," Jenna said.

I laughed, shaking my head at my crazy volleyball friends. They were definitely a lot of fun. I would miss them if I left the team in a couple of weeks.

How was I going to decide?

View from the Bleachers

T hanks for the ride, Mrs. Tanaka," I said, climbing into the back seat.

"You're welcome, Elle," she said. "It's nice that you and Blake want to cheer on your friends."

"Yeah, nice that Blake wants to cheer on his g—"

Blake turned around and punched my arm before I could say "girlfriend." I figured out right then that his mom didn't know he had one.

"—his good friends," I finished, and then I made a face at Blake.

When we got to Spring Meadow, I repaid Blake

for his punch in the arm. "So, your mom doesn't know that Bianca is your girlfriend?" I asked.

"Well, she's not *officially* my girlfriend," he replied. "But yeah, my mom doesn't know that we like each other. I think she might freak out. Or ask a bunch of questions."

"She'll figure it out sooner or later," I told him. "Your mom's pretty smart."

"I know," he admitted. "But I'm going to see how long I can go."

I shook my head, laughing, and we walked inside the gym. The Nighthawks were warming up on one side of the court in their green and yellow uniforms. On the other side, girls in red and white uniforms— the Cardinals—took turns shooting at the basket.

We made our way to the home side of the stands. Caroline's brother Pete was there with their mom, and he scooted across the bleachers when he saw me.

"Elle! Elle! Are you going to play today?"

I shook my head. "No, I just came here to cheer on the team," I told him.

Pete frowned.

"Hey, we can cheer Caroline together," I said. "Will you help me cheer Caroline?"

He nodded and cupped his hands around his mouth. "Go, Caroline!"

"Go, Caroline!" I echoed.

His sister looked up at the stands and smiled and waved at us. Then my other friends did too. Even Bianca waved, although I'm pretty sure she was waving at Blake, and not me.

I nervously tapped my foot as Coach Ramirez gathered the team in a huddle. *Who is she going to put in first?* I wondered. *What kind of defense is she using?*

The huddle broke apart and five Nighthawks moved onto the court. Coach had started Bianca as center, Avery as point guard, Hannah as shooting guard, Tiff as power forward, and Dina as small forward.

Bianca and the Cardinals center went to half court for the tip-off. The ref blew his whistle and tossed the ball in the air. Bianca shot up like a rocket and batted it to Avery.

Avery tore down the court, dodging the Cardinals defense.

"Go, go, go!" I cheered.

Avery made it all the way to the basket! She took a shot, but it bounced off the backboard. Luckily, Hannah was right there to rebound it. She grabbed it and tossed it in before the Cardinals defense could block her shot.

"Two points!" Pete yelled next to me, and Blake and I whooped and cheered.

From my seat in the stands I had a view of the team I'd never seen before—way different even from watching the game when I was benched. From the stands I could see how the whole team worked together. I could see how Dina would always aggressively go for the ball, and how Hannah always seemed a tiny bit unsure of where to be on the court. And how Bianca didn't like to pass and always tried to take the shot herself.

It also became really clear that the Nighthawks needed to work on their defense. The Cardinals scored three baskets that first quarter!

"They need better teamwork out there," I whispered to Blake, and he nodded.

In the second quarter Bianca helped to lessen the gap with a score from the three-point zone. But it was Patrice, who came in for Dina, who was the most surprising. She was more confident on the court than I'd ever seen her! I'm not sure if she was feeling better already, or if she was just more confident because she had talked things out with her mom. Whatever the reason, she made some really great moves.

Tiff passed her the ball and one of the Cardinal defenders was all over her. But Patrice executed a beautiful pivot and passed the ball to Avery, who had nobody guarding her. Avery sank two points.

"Aveeerrry!" I cheered. Then I added. "Nice move, Patrice!"

"Yeah, nice move!" Pete repeated.

But my biggest surprise came in the third quarter. There's a rule that no player can play all four quarters, so I knew that someone would have to sub in for Bianca as center. I wasn't expecting it to be Amanda!

It's not that Amanda's a bad player. But she's not one of our taller players. And she's also the least experienced member of the team.

"Woo-hoo! You can do it, Amanda!" I yelled.

To start the half, the center for the Cardinals took the ball to throw in, and Amanda ran to cover her. The girl was six inches taller than Amanda, but Amanda jumped up really high to guard her as the Cardinal passed the ball to her teammate. I literally gasped as Amanda grabbed the ball in midair!

"Whoa!" I said.

"That was pretty cool," Blake remarked. "She was gonna get that ball, no matter what!"

"And she got it!" I said, and Blake and I high-fived.

The Nighthawks tied up the game by the end of the third quarter, 18–18. As the fourth quarter began, I realized I was on the edge of my seat. It was anybody's game.

My right foot began to tap more furiously on the bleachers. My whole body was itching to get in there and play! Blake sensed it.

"Am I going to have to hold you back?" he asked.

"You might," I said. I really wanted to be out there, suited up and ready to join my teammates!

When the fourth quarter started, the Cardinals took the ball down the court for an easy two points. Avery took the ball and passed it on to Patrice, who dribbled a few feet and then passed it to Caroline. She dribbled a few feet and passed it to Bianca. Three Cardinals surrounded her.

I bit my lip, watching. What would Bianca do? She could try to jump higher than all of them and make the basket. Or she could pass to Avery, who was open, but how would she get the ball past them?

Bianca faked a pass. Then she faked again. And then, while the Cardinals were confused, she jumped up and made the shot! Three points!

"Biaaaaaaaaanca!" Blake and I cheered, and Pete joined in.

The Nighthawks didn't keep their lead for long. The Cardinals scored another two points a few minutes later. Then the two teams traded the ball back and forth until the clock started winding down.

There was less than a minute left in the game, and the Cardinals were up by a point. Bianca had the ball, and Patrice was wide open.

"Bianca, look around you!" Coach Ramirez called out.

Bianca spotted Patrice just as a Cardinals defender charged toward her. She made the pass. Patrice caught it, brought it closer to the basket, and shot it in for two points.

Seconds later, the ref's whistle blew.

"Nighthawks win!" Pete yelled.

Patrice was beaming. She ran to her mom, who grabbed her in a big hug. I was on my feet, clapping and cheering like crazy.

"That game was intense," I said. "So much action!"

"Yeah, it was," Blake said. "Did you see Bianca out there? The Cardinals didn't know what to expect."

My heart was pounding, as if I'd been playing on the court with them. It had been an awesome game. And then I thought, if I can feel that way on the stands, could I feel the same joy again if I was on the court?

I headed down to the court and found Amanda. Her cheeks were pink from the game, making her freckles stand out.

"You played center!" I said.

She grinned. "Yeah, well, nobody wanted to do it," she said, "and I volunteered, so Coach said she'd give me a shot. I know I can never fill your shoes, Elle, but . . ."

"You did great!" I told her. "You never gave up that ball easily. And you put your whole heart into it. That's what matters."

"Thanks," she said.

Then I felt a tap on my shoulder.

"Can we talk for a minute?"

It was Bianca.

"Sure," I said, and she pulled me over to the sidelines.

"So, Elle," she said, and she was staring down at her sneakers. "I'm sorry if I gave you a hard time when you were on the team."

I was surprised, even though I knew that Natalie had promised to talk to her.

"Thanks," I said.

"If you come back to the team, it'll be different," Bianca promised. "I mean, we won't be best friends or anything, but . . . it'll be cool this time. Okay?"

"No name-calling?" I asked, and she shook her head.

I knew this wasn't easy for her to do. But I also felt like I could believe her.

"Thanks," I said, and then I decided to deal with the whole reason why she'd been mad at me in the first place. "You know that I never asked to play center, right?"

"I know," she said. "It just killed me not to play it anymore. But I'm over it. I just want us to play our best. And win."

"I'm still not sure if I want to rejoin the team," I told her. "But thanks. This helps."

"We need you, Elle," Bianca said, and then she walked away.

Natalie ran up to me. "How'd it go?"

"Good," I replied. "Thanks for talking to her."

"No problem," Natalie said. "You should come celebrate with us, Elle. We're getting pizza."

Amanda had walked up, and she overheard. "Yeah, my mom can give you and Blake a ride home. He says he's coming too."

I smiled. "Sure. I'll text my mom."

"Nighthawks! Team meeting before you head out for pizza!" Coach Ramirez yelled.

Instinctively, I moved toward Coach with the others before I stopped myself. I wasn't part of the team anymore. But I was starting to think that I could be a Nighthawk again. I went over the last few weeks in my head.

Trying out new things . . . check!

Bianca problem solved . . . check!

Realizing I could have fun playing basketball if I didn't put pressure on myself . . . big check!

Working things out with Coach Ramirez . . .

The team meeting broke up, and Avery ran over to me.

"I heard you're coming for pizza. Awesome!" she said.

"Yeah," I said, and I glanced back at Coach Ramirez as we jogged out of the gym.

I'd have to talk to Coach. It had worked for Patrice, so maybe it would work for me, too.

And if things went well, then maybe, just maybe, I could be one of the Nighthawks again!